VET IN DEMAND

For Elissa Hart, the shock of her father's sudden death is bad enough. To find his veterinary practice in such a poor state, both financially and with dated equipment, is just as upsetting. The only way to save the practice is to take on a partner able to make a real investment — and Adam Kennedy is willing to do just that. Can Elissa reconcile her resentment of Adam and his bold ideas with her growing attraction to him?

CAROL WOOD

VET IN DEMAND

Complete and Unabridged

LINFORD
Leicester

First published in Great Britain

First Linford Edition
published 2014

All the characters in this book have no
existence outside the imagination of the
author, and have no relation whatsoever
to anyone bearing the same name or names.
They are not even distantly inspired by any
individual known or unknown to the author,
and all the incidents are pure invention.

A catalogue record for this book is available
from the British Library.

ISBN 978–1–4448–1939–7

Published by
F.A. Thorpe (Publishing)
Anstey, Leicestershire

Set by Words & Graphics Ltd.
Anstey, Leicestershire
Printed and bound in Great Britain by
T. J. International Ltd., Padstow, Cornwall

This book is printed on acid-free paper

1

Elissa took a deep breath and opened Trinka's cage . . . carefully.

Innocence personified, thought Elissa, unable to suppress a grin at the little chimpanzee who stared back at her with immense marble-black eyes. 'Come along, mischief,' she coaxed, 'the sooner we get those teeth sorted out, the better.'

Trinka grinned a brown, toothy grin, curling back her lips. Then she exploded like a firework. A gaggle of hairy arms and legs burst into life, charging the half-open door, thrusting the frame against Elissa's cheekbone with a resounding crack.

Elissa saw stars. She also saw the acrobatic form of Trinka swing on to the top of Honeybunch's pen where, clapping her palms together, she gleefully bared her teeth at the lion cub below.

Honeybunch emitted a growled yawn. Sleepily he mustered up enough energy to flick a fat paw at the strong wire mesh, gnashing his cub's teeth. Trinka howled with delight above, dangling a bony finger down through the mesh, grinning malevolently.

Elissa sighed, rubbing her cheek, feeling as though her face had doubled its size. 'We haven't time for games, Trinka. Grace will be here any moment . . . and you want your pre-med done before she arrives, don't you?'

Trinka shook her head furiously. She gave another ear-piercing screech and flapped her long arms like wings. Then, horror of horrors, she disappeared into the next room.

By the time Elissa cornered her again in Theatre, she was dangling from the flexible arm of the ancient dental machine extended over the operating table.

Elissa sighed, pushing a curly golden-brown strand of hair from her eyes. 'Trinka, be a good girl . . . Come to me . . . please?'

No hope, thought Elissa, as the mischievous chimpanzee scooped a stethoscope from the trolley, launched it through the air like a javelin and beat her breast as it turned a double somersault and fell with a slap on the floor.

To both Trinka's and Elissa's surprise, the instrument lay just inches away from a large pair of well-heeled brogue shoes, which, it appeared, had just stepped over the threshold.

'I seem to have arrived at a rather inconvenient time,' said the stranger, with a smile. Bending to pick up the instrument, he inspected it and added cheerfully as he handed it back, 'No damage done, fortunately.'

He was extremely tall, ebony-haired and dressed in a perfectly tailored dark suit, despite the fact, reflected Elissa, that it was June and un-Britishly warm for the time of year.

He smiled again, quite a stunning smile, under a tan which made her own dusky skin colour look pale by contrast.

'My name is Kennedy, by the way,' he added briskly. 'Adam Kennedy.'

Of course, she should have known! She should have recognised the voice at least, the lazy, deep drawl which had drifted over the phone three or four days ago in answer to her advertisement in the *Veterinary Record*.

'I think,' said Adam Kennedy, glancing behind her, 'our friend is about to take off . . . '

Elissa swivelled on her heel just in time to see Trinka leap from the flexible arm to the washbasin. With great resourcefulness, she coaxed on a tap, plunging the tip of her finger into its nozzle.

Despite the deluge, Adam Kennedy stroked the water from his face, smiling, then calmly removed his jacket, held it firmly by the collar and braved yet another torrent of water to aim it perfectly over an astonished Trinka.

Elissa blinked hard at the sight of the broad, tightly muscled shoulders moving like lightning beneath the expensive blue

4

shirt. Trinka was in his arms before she could blink again. 'It's not every day I have the pleasure of holding such a charming young lady in my arms,' he laughed and, as he broadened his grin, Elissa almost forgot what she was about.

'I — er — I want to give her a pre-med for a dental op, you see,' she began hurriedly, managing to fill the syringe. 'It's those canines . . . I intend to try to level them off.'

'Yes, I can see what you mean. What's her history?'

Elissa sighed. 'She's really very tame, but she's taken to nipping her keeper at the local wildlife park just outside Farwell. They don't want to put her in with the mainstream monkeys, of course . . . yet leaving her in the children's section is far too dangerous now.'

Adam Kennedy met Trinka's anarchic gaze with amusement while Elissa injected the tranquilliser into her thigh, and very soon the little chimp subsided, albeit reluctantly, into the circle of the powerfully gentle arms.

Her visitor was handsome in a streamlined kind of way, Elissa decided, as she stared at him under her auburn lashes — not the type to be interested in Larkhill at all. He had given his age as thirty-two — seven years older than herself — was surprisingly unmarried, and had turned out to be the son of Victor Kennedy, the renowned London ophthalmic surgeon. Adam was a consultant ophthalmologist himself, which made his interest in a rural, unsophisticated practice surprising to say the least.

Adam Kennedy's gaze shifted over the room. He nodded at the overhead dental arm. 'Good grief! Where did you dig that antique up from?'

Elissa stiffened. 'The machine is adequate, Mr Kennedy, if old. My father used it for many years and found it very satisfactory.'

Elissa hesitated, as in a rush of remembrance the ache flooded back with fresh intensity. A month had passed since her father's death. Four nightmare weeks.

First, the news of his fatal coronary while she was on holiday in France, then, on her return, the discovery that the practice was in dire straits.

'I'm sure he did, Miss Hart.' Adam Kennedy seemed to pick up her train of thought. 'I was sorry to hear of your loss.'

She nodded, wishing Grace would materialise. It was extremely unusual for Grace not to turn up on time, and it had to be today of all days. 'My assistant will be here soon, I hope,' she said quickly, aware that he was laying Trinka gently down on the operating table. 'If you'd care to wait?' She glanced at her watch. 'Though it is only two and I wasn't expecting you until five.'

'I must apologise,' he murmured, pensively frowning down at Trinka. 'I arrived last night and booked in at the Saracen in Farwell. Since it's such a beautiful day, I'm afraid I couldn't resist taking a look around.'

Elissa was aware, under the intense dark gaze, of how dishevelled she was.

Her naturally wavy mop of golden auburn hair needing washing, a job she was reserving until after Trinka's op. Her jeans had seen better days, as had her white Kenyan T-shirt with a conservation park logo on the front. All this she would have remedied though, before her meeting with Adam Kennedy.

'I can't think what's happened to Grace — my father's assistant. It's so unlike her to be late,' Elissa sighed distractedly.

'May I help?' He arched persuasive dark eyebrows. 'Now the pre-med has been given, it seems senseless to delay.'

'Oh . . . ' Elissa wondered why she felt suddenly under pressure. 'I wouldn't put you to the trouble.'

'Absolutely none.'

She was reluctant to accept, yet she knew that if Grace didn't turn up, the operation would be twice as tricky on her own.

'I'll scrub up,' she agreed finally, 'in the prep-room just through here.' She gestured to an adjoining room which her father had used for theatre preparation, and left him, vaguely aware of the slow movements of the large, tanned hands, the gentle way he held Trinka's little brown fingers over his, the swift and automatic movement of his own to her pulse.

While she was changing, Elissa's mind worked hectically. Adam Kennedy was obviously highly motivated, just returning, he'd explained, from five years of practice in Los Angeles. Buying into a country practice in the middle of Shropshire surely wasn't his cup of tea? Yet here he was, the third and last of the responses she had had to her advertisement in the *Veterinary Record* — and three hours early too!

Elissa walked into Theatre, her mane of curls tucked well into her cap, her slender five feet seven hidden under the surgical gown, her large green eyes wide and alert above the dark, grieving circles of the last few weeks.

'A set of my father's greens are in the prep-room if you would like to use

9

them,' she suggested, and felt the sad ache of awareness that another man would now be wearing them.

Trinka took the anaesthetic well, and Elissa watched as Adam gently opened the little black mouth for her. Peering in at the teeth, she pointed to the offending fangs. 'I'm going to saw the canines flush with the gums and round them off, so restricting the chances of her doing any serious damage.'

His mask was drawn across the firm, well-shaped mouth which had so struck her earlier when he smiled. Only the dark eyes stared at her compellingly.

Her attention shifted down to Trinka and she set about levelling the first canine. Adam Kennedy meanwhile regulated the anaesthetic machine, checking respiration and watching Elissa in silence, passing her the necessary tools.

'Denervation next.' Elissa referred to the large dental canals. 'Trinka's roots don't end in a point as they do with humans, of course, but they're broad and flat.'

He moved beside her and Elissa was aware of a change in atmosphere as he murmured, 'You need vastly more up-to-date equipment, don't you?'

She glanced at him. 'That's true. But I'm doing the best I can with the resources I have for the moment.'

'Indeed you are,' he returned swiftly.

With increasing anguish after this remark, she continued to perform the nerve extraction with the ex-hospital dental equipment her father had cherished for years. She was forced to admit that he was right. Larkhill was embarrassingly outdated — but did he need to remind her of it in such a smug fashion?

'And your plans for new equipment?' he persisted. 'You must have some?'

'I hope to discuss refurbishment with my new . . . with a potential partner,' Elissa evaded, trying not to sound as defensive as she felt.

'Ah,' he said with a sigh. 'In other words you need capital urgently.'

She straightened her back and fixed

him with her sparkling green eyes. 'If you really want to know, Mr Kennedy, I could have had financial help from another vet, a close friend of my father's, who is also my godfather. But though the offer was tempting, I refused. I want independence. I want Larkhill on its feet. And I want a partner to help me.'

Was there a ghost of amusement in his eyes? Elissa wondered as she took a breath. If there was, it was gone in an instant as he said soberly, 'I admire your tenacity.'

'Tenacity costs nothing,' Elissa observed, returning her attention to disinfecting Trinka's exposed canals. 'But new equipment does, of course.'

Why did he irritate her so much? It was a bad start indeed and, despite his able assistance, Elissa wished she had refused his help even at the cost of delaying the operation.

'May we drop the formalities?' he asked. 'It's Adam.'

She nodded. 'Elissa,' she muttered.

'Cement, please.'

He passed it. 'You've done this op before?'

'Not with chimpanzees. But with other animals — hyenas. I was with the Overseas Development Administration working in Kenya for eighteen months after qualifying. Our work involved studies tracking certain species, taking blood samples and testing for serious diseases.'

'You enjoyed it?'

'Immensely.'

'And you didn't consider the option of joining your father after qualifying? I'm sure with a few bright ideas from a young woman like yourself the place wouldn't have deteriorated to such an extent.'

Elissa turned angrily now, his insensitive remark making her gasp. She pulled down her mask. 'I really don't think my motives for going abroad are any of your concern! And I resent the implication of neglect. My father was dedicated to animals, they were his

13

priority, and if he happened to put them first before — '

'Hey . . . hey!' He raised his hands, shaking his head slowly, then, pulling down his mask too, he added, 'I'm sorry I've upset you. I realise this must be a sensitive time . . . but I'm not criticising your father — or you. He was perfectly entitled to his opinion — and his way of life. But the equipment you've been using leaves a lot be desired and, though your skill and resourcefulness in using it is beyond reproach, this is not the way an efficient veterinary business is run today.' He gave a shrug. 'Perhaps I must make myself clear. I'll be quite blunt. I would want to make decisive changes if I bought into this practice. Eventually, I'd like to specialise in ophthalmology and set up a special referral unit.'

They stood in silence. Elissa felt like telling this arrogant stranger that she hadn't the least interest in his ideas on lucrative, efficient veterinary practices! But, unfortunately, his comments were plainly sound, besides which she couldn't risk losing yet another interested party.

'I see,' she answered tightly. 'I don't think I have any reservations . . . but it's a new idea. I'd have to think about it.'

He nodded. 'There's no rush, anyway. Whether you would want to incorporate a theatre within Larkhill, or perhaps adjoining it, if we could obtain planning permission . . . ? And as for Larkhill itself, I'd like to see the surgery redecorated and new equipment brought in immediately . . . which I am quite happy to finance, if we can reach amicable terms?'

He was right, of course. Even the small tools were out of date, wonderfully preserved, but inexcusably ancient. Oh, Dad, she thought suddenly in deep dismay, why didn't I see you were struggling? Was I so absorbed with my life that I couldn't see what was happening in yours?

Much later, in recovery, when they had both disrobed and Trinka was coming round on a drip, Adam Kennedy touched her lightly on her shoulder. 'Do you know you have rather a spectacular bruise on your cheek?'

Elissa felt a fierce flush of colour and put up her hand. But his fingers were there before hers and his touch startled her.

'I . . . The cage door . . . I didn't move out of the way quickly enough,' she stammered, aware that he was turning her chin to the light.

He smiled. 'The only positive remark I can find to make about the damage is that it enhances the vivid green of your lovely eyes. If you had to have a bruise, this one's definitely a perfect colour match.'

She looked at him hesitantly, then, as he began to laugh, she laughed too.

Slowly he dropped his fingers. She was holding her breath under his intense gaze when suddenly the phone rang in the office. Elissa hurried to answer it, grateful for the opportunity to leave her visitor's disturbing presence.

Grace's voice came breathlessly over the phone. Her car had broken down and was being towed to the local garage at Farwell where they were going to fit a new battery. At least one mystery was solved!

Pausing to think after replacing the phone, Elissa finally went back to the recovery-room. 'Your jacket — did Trinka damage it?' she asked, as he examined a shivering Trinka.

He smiled, displaying the even white teeth under the solid tan, his face framed by black, glossy hair cut smoothly away from his lean face. 'Not at all. I left it to dry by the radiator. Look, if you're going to stay with your patient, would you mind me wandering around the surgery on my own and taking a look?'

Elissa still couldn't get used to the sense of invasion she was feeling. 'If you wish,' she agreed somewhat coolly. 'When Trinka's fully round I'll come and find you. Grace will be in by then. Her car broke down, but she said she would leave it at the garage and come in by bus. Farwell centre is only ten minutes or so away.'

He walked to the radiator, picked up his jacket and slid it on over broad shoulders. 'Is there somewhere we could eat in Farwell this evening?' he asked without preamble. 'I think perhaps we would both benefit from a good meal before we talk business.'

He'd caught her completely unawares and, for a moment, she was lost for words. Talking business sounded positive, but she didn't want to become over-hopeful, nor did she want to waste time if he was at a loose end before returning to London.

'Don't look so worried,' he laughed lightly. 'I'm simply a hungry man, who is genuinely interested in Larkhill. And — er — we might iron out one or two differences of opinion without coming to blows if we are safely anchored down on neutral territory.'

Elissa smiled ruefully. 'Put like that, I can't refuse. I think the carvery at The Shropshire Lad if you don't want to eat at the hotel.'

He nodded and glanced at Trinka.

'She's going to be sore, but she's coming along just fine. Well done. You did a great job.' For a moment he remained perfectly still, staring at her, and she caught the flare of admiration in his eyes, their depths inky black and swirling with an exotic and exciting intensity which he took no pains to hide. The moment passed, leaving her feeling curiously ill at ease.

After he was gone, Elissa bent to listen to Trinka's heartbeat and had to pull back. Her own blood drummed so heavily in her ears that it made the task quite impossible.

When Grace finally arrived in her mended car and took over Trinka's care, Elissa toured her guest round the rambling Larkhill her grandfather had built. The surgery had been added as an extension with a connecting door in the fifties, but the house, to both her pride and regret, hadn't changed a bit in all those years.

The rustic staircase leading up to the first floor still creaked on every stair and positively groaned as she led the way up it.

'This first floor,' she explained, 'would be entirely the new practice partner's. Although it's not self-contained, I rarely need to use the staircase except perhaps occasionally to go into what we call the loft — two small rooms at the top of the house which are never used and are filled with rubbish.'

Elissa pushed open the first door to display a very large room with comfortable furniture scattered about it: a writing-desk and sofa and a beautiful walnut dining-table under which were pushed four high-backed chairs and a carver's chair.

'This floor has been little used since my mother's death,' she said with a sigh. 'I'm sorry, it must smell rather stuffy.'

'Not at all.' Her companion stared around the room.

'I wasn't at home very much, so Dad found the downstairs more than enough for his needs. Both floors have very large rooms.'

'Most elegant,' Adam remarked, with obvious admiration. 'I've yet to invest in much furniture because I've been on the move so much. But this — this is really quite delightful.'

'I'm afraid there are no cooking facilities here,' she added hesitantly. 'But there is a very substantial kitchen on the ground floor. Grace came in every weekday morning to help my father in the house and surgery. She used to cook breakfast for him and prepare an evening meal. I'm afraid she still does so for me . . . Doubtless we could come to some arrangement.'

'Excellent,' Adam remarked positively.

He looked in each of the three other rooms, glancing around them approvingly, smiling at the stately double bed and walnut veneer bedroom suite.

Finally they came to the flat's bathroom and the original Victorian white enamel bath, dwarfed by the high ceiling. Adam glanced from the long sash window to the garden beneath.

'What a beautiful garden.'

Elissa nodded, going to stand beside him. 'It is rather, isn't it?' She smiled wistfully. 'You can see the kennels to the left of the old grass tennis-court. There's even a stable. As a child, I had a small pony called Red. Dad taught me to ride, mostly in the woods across the road, along the bridle-paths.'

'Lucky girl,' he said, turning his attention back to her, 'to grow up in such an environment. You had no brothers or sisters?'

Elissa shook her head. 'No, but there were always animals. I never wanted for company.'

They stood in silence for a while as the sun dipped below the trees in the garden and cast long shadows over the emerald lawn. Eventually they walked into the hall and he took a last look round before they descended the staircase. 'So much space. Lots of character. I like it very much.'

Elissa raised curious eyebrows. 'You do?'

He laughed. 'Why so surprised?'

She shrugged. 'I'm not sure. As I was showing you the house I just felt, seeing it through someone else's eyes, it must look rather dull and old-fashioned.'

He shook his head slowly. 'No, not to me. I think the house has a kind of timeless quality about it.' He smiled wryly at her expression of surprise. 'But . . . let's finish the tour. Perhaps if you'll just show me the kitchen?'

Somewhat taken aback, Elissa headed for the stone-flagged kitchen. Grace had set the vast pine table with a vase of flowers, roses and maidenhair from the garden. The place was as clean as a new pin. Through the window they could see once again the spilling flowerbeds and unused tennis-court speckled with dandelions.

Turning to her companion, she saw that he was captivated.

*   *   *

It was a unique, if somewhat neglected, property and Adam Kennedy remarked as much as they enjoyed a traditional English roast that evening at The Shropshire Lad. 'I'm intrigued,' he drawled, running a satisfied hand over a blade-flat abdomen as he leaned back in his chair after the meal. 'You've been entirely frank. The practice is in trouble, but I have to ask, why didn't your father take some professional financial advice and put the business back on its feet? Or if not, surely your godfather would have been able to help?'

Elissa shook her head. 'Dad was far too proud to ask for help. Harry Fitzroy had no idea of the seriousness of the situation until after Dad's death.'

Elissa had just survived a very difficult hour. She had decided to admit the financial problems before Adam Kennedy's accountants reviewed the figures and gave him the fright of his life! Now he was entitled to ask her questions. It was simply that she couldn't find the answers to give him.

'Dad never quite recovered after my

mother's death ten years ago,' she endeavoured to explain. 'I assumed it was his angina and I suppose I was relieved he didn't hare around to aggravate it.' She sighed deeply. 'Perhaps if I hadn't gone abroad after my training and I'd come straight into the practice, then I wouldn't have taken the holiday in France. The problem was, it was a holiday I had planned with a girlfriend from college and I didn't want to let her down.' She paused as she remembered, with an aching feeling inside her. 'I came across a handful of unpaid invoices just before I left. I began to suspect something was wrong. When I confronted Dad he insisted I shouldn't worry. He said everything was being taken care of. I just wish . . . '

'I'm sure your father didn't want to worry you with the predicament he was in before you left,' Adam suggested reasonably. 'I think he was delaying telling you until after you came back. After all, if he had gone into details before you left, I expect you would have cancelled, wouldn't you?'

She nodded. 'Yes, of course!'

Suddenly his hand slipped across the table, covering hers. 'I shouldn't have brought up the subject. Would you like me to take you home?'

She shook her head. 'No. I'm fine. Really.'

'Hang on in there,' he smiled. 'Time really is the most effective cure.' For a while he left his hand over hers, then, rather stiffly, he drew away.

The skin of her hand where his fingers had rested tingled and grew warm. Swallowing, she cleared her throat. 'Since Mum's illness and death, Dad really hadn't any incentive. I suppose I was too preoccupied with my own life to notice anything was seriously wrong. After qualifying at Bristol, I managed to secure a place with the ODA which enabled me to travel as I'd always wanted.' She shrugged. 'Though the prospect of settling down in practice at Larkhill was always in my mind . . . it seemed a long way off in those days. I suppose I always imagined Dad and I had the future ahead of us.'

She reclined back in her chair, frowning slightly. Would this man understand? And as she stared at him, at the elegant way he was dressed this evening in a black jacket and crisp white shirt, his black hair smoothed back and his dark eyes very astute, his life obviously so well-ordered and secure, she had her doubts. Yet she had talked more to him in one day than she had talked to anyone since her father's death. True, it was with a view to salvaging the business; Adam Kennedy was her best prospect yet. But there was something about him, about those deep, dark eyes, which invited confidences.

She realised too that she had taken more trouble with her appearance this evening, more than at any time since the funeral. Of course, she flaunted the huge bruise on her cheek which she'd had to disguise with make-up, but it didn't detract from the dress of

turquoise silk which she had resur-
rected from her wardrobe. She had
even had the enthusiasm to team the
greeny-blue with the golden heart on a
delicate chain which her mother had
bought her for her fifteenth birthday.

She gazed fondly at the bracelet on
her wrist, a present from her father in
celebration of her Finals. Unconsciously
she seemed to have worn all these
things as lucky charms. She wondered if
Adam Kennedy would prove to be
lucky too.

His coffee drunk, he leaned both
elbows on the table and contemplated
her. 'You've had others to view the
practice?' he asked bluntly.

She nodded. 'Two, actually. One
wanted to bring his young family to
Larkhill. He has three children and
another on the way.' Elissa smiled
ruefully, her green eyes twinkling. 'Of
course there is masses of room, it would
be ideal for them, but I'm not quite
sure I'm prepared for . . . '

'A ready-made family?' he grinned,

the dark eyes roaming her face.

Elissa nodded. 'I love children. I would like a family of my own one day, but . . . '

'But the day hasn't yet dawned?'

She felt uncomfortable now. They were straying from the subject of the practice. And she felt as though she had revealed enough about herself for one night to a man who, after all her efforts, might turn round and say simply, thanks, but no thanks!

'The other interested party,' she said firmly, ignoring his question, 'was another female vet. I liked her very much. We agreed tentatively.' Elissa sighed at the memory of the disappointment. 'Unfortunately she changed her mind at the last minute.'

He smiled. 'A woman's prerogative, so they say.'

Elissa studied him carefully, detecting a slight cynicism in his voice. 'I would have been delighted to have another female partner!'

'An all-female practice?' He scowled.

'The boot certainly seems to be on the other foot these days as regards discrimination!'

Elissa felt her temper rise, very swiftly, very decidedly. 'Mr Kennedy,' she said coldly, reaching down for her handbag, making it plain their time was up, 'it's no longer entirely a man's world, or haven't you noticed?'

He caught her wrist as she began to get up. 'It's Adam, Elissa. Do you have any problem with calling me by my Christian name?' The strength in his grip took her breath away as she sat down again.

They stared at one another, her green eyes challenging.

'No problem at all,' she answered crisply, 'providing you are genuinely interested in Larkhill.'

He watched her, his eyes pensive. But there was no hesitation in his voice as he said, 'In which case, Elissa, subject to my accountants reviewing the figures and to your full agreement on my plans for a referral unit, I'll instruct my solicitor to contact yours and begin negotiations immediately.'

She opened her mouth to speak, but discovered that, because of the shock, she couldn't say a word.

He smiled. 'If you're happy with this, I'd like to move in as soon as possible. I really think we should lose no time in putting Larkhill back on the map again.'

2

'Elissa?'

There was a momentary pause as Elissa gripped the telephone tighter. 'Yes . . . Adam . . . how are you?'

'Extremely well.' The unhesitating reply caused Elissa's heart to pound faster. 'You've heard from my solicitors?'

Elissa had not only had full communication from her own solicitor over the past ten days, but had to her astonishment realised that, with breathtaking efficiency, Adam Kennedy had now financially sealed his commitment to Larkhill as her practice partner. 'Yes,' she murmured, trying to allay the unsettled feeling in her stomach. 'There was no problem as far as I was concerned. All the paperwork should be going through.'

'In which case,' she heard, as his

voice came lightly over the phone, 'I was hoping, if possible, to move in next Saturday. Would that be convenient?'

Elissa felt her stomach lurch. She tried to puzzle out why, with everything going her way, she should feel so apprehensive. 'Next Saturday,' she repeated, her mind spinning.

'If it isn't convenient . . .'

'I have an open surgery until twelve. After that, yes . . . why not?'

Now, a week later, as she stared out of the surgery window remembering that phone call and awaiting his arrival, Elissa distractedly stroked Jemima, her father's British Blue cat, who was balancing on the windowsill. Though Jemima would not be lifted into her arms, she purred noisily as she too seemed to sense an arrival. A ripple of electricity went through the thick blue-grey hair under her fingers, as a car Elissa recognised slipped smoothly into the drive.

Jemima jumped down to the floor and scuttled off in disdain of yet another visitor. Elissa's heart thudded as she watched Adam Kennedy climb out of his car. Dressed in thigh-hugging denims and navy polo sweater, he walked towards the surgery from the steel-grey Mercedes with the latest registration plates which, she reflected wryly, put her father's hatchback into the definable category of antique.

Elissa took a deep breath and went to meet him. A summer breeze blew in as she stood in the open doorway under a froth of pink and white honeysuckle.

'Hello!' he greeted her warmly. 'I've been having my doubts as to whether I've rushed you, asking to move in so soon. I think we must have completed the swiftest transaction in history!'

She smiled. 'Yes, I was rather surprised.' She looked back to the Mercedes. 'Can I help with your luggage?'

Adam thrust a large hand through his hair. 'I've very little, actually. Just essentials. The removers are bringing my ophthalmic equipment and a few pieces of furniture next week. I hope it won't disrupt routine too much.'

'I expect we'll survive,' Elissa smiled, also secretly hoping it wouldn't disrupt too much. She presented him with a bunch of keys. 'I've tagged them all, so you'll know which keys are for which.' She gestured for him to enter. 'Can I offer you some lunch?'

'As a matter of fact I ate *en route*.' He hesitated briefly, glancing around the room. 'What I would really like to do, if you've time, is to go through the surgery, talk about the kind of redecoration we want. And new equipment — now that's first on our list, don't you think?'

Elissa frowned. 'I'd imagined you would need a few days to settle in.'

He shrugged dismissively. 'Oh, no . . . I'm sure I'll find my way around perfectly well.' Frowning at the dull ochre walls and chocolate paint of the waiting-room, he studied the room. 'I think white walls and wainscoting in here to freshen it up, and — ' he took her arm, guiding her through into the hall ' — in here, we could install overhead lighting and some good strong durable flooring. What about having each treatment-room in colour co-ordinated pastels to give relief to the eye? What do you think?'

Elissa hardly had time to catch her breath. 'To be honest, I hadn't given it a great deal of thought as yet.' She shrugged, giving a little sigh. 'The place is gloomy, I'll admit.'

'No problem at all,' Adam smiled, rubbing his chin as he looked towards the theatres. 'Structurally I can see the building is in good shape. A few coats of emulsion will make all the difference. Now . . . what about equipment for the two theatres?' He walked ahead as Elissa followed. 'We need new operating tables, obviously — and the old anaesthetic machine should be replaced by a portable one.' Grinning at the dental machine, he laughed. 'I remember that thing! We need a much more modern one, of course!'

She felt a prickle of irritation as he patrolled the theatre, picking up some of the instruments and replacing them. Elissa wondered why she felt so reluctant to replace her father's beloved equipment when it was common sense to do so, and, trying to dismiss her unease, she shrugged lightly. 'I don't suppose there's too much rush,' she murmured hopefully. 'We've managed so far for years with what Dad had. A few more weeks isn't going to do any harm.'

He looked at her in surprise. 'Oh, I had a fair idea of what we wanted from my last visit. I've already spoken to the company who supply the latest medical equipment and they can hurry through an order for us just as soon as we let them have the details.' Then, smiling broadly again, he walked into the theatre and made calculations on a scrap of paper, tucking the slip into his jeans pocket. One thick, dark eyebrow tilted up as he turned towards her. 'Which is why I thought taking the bull by both horns today would save us a lot of time and energy next week when we'll both be trying to establish practice procedure.'

There was that dry cynicism in his voice which she had noticed before. She tried not to bridle at it, reminding herself that what he had said was perfectly true, and walked with him in silence to the consulting-room her father had always used.

'We have this and two other rooms which are ideal for consultations, don't we?' he murmured vaguely. 'Each could do with a new bench, especially this one. It's rather battered, isn't it?'

Elissa stiffened. 'This bench was my father's. I'm sure I'll manage perfectly with it.'

He nodded. 'Naturally . . . Sentimental value.' Looking at her with a frown, he added, 'I'm afraid I was thoughtless.' He moved to the door quietly, rubbing a large hand over his chin. 'Shall we start on the office and reception equipment?'

Elissa moved out of the room, her heart increasing its beat with what now seemed like regular familiarity every time Adam brought up a refurbishment idea. He was obviously trying to include her and she should be more ready to exchange ideas. But getting used to a very different male presence from her father's at Larkhill was going to be even more difficult than she had imagined.

Trying to make an effort, Elissa gestured towards the uncomfortable waiting-room chairs. 'These need to be replaced and we need a comprehensive list of our prices on the wall, so people can see our charges at a glance.'

Adam nodded and made yet another note on his piece of paper. In the office, which was overflowing with papers and veterinary books which Elissa had not had time to go through, she apologised for the mess.

Adam frowned. 'Shelf-space and files for a start?'

Elissa looked round the familiar room, cluttered with her father's things, and nodded. 'Dad was never particularly organised. He used to say it was organised chaos.'

'Some people can work like that,' Adam agreed with a wry smile. 'But I prefer to leave all the hard work to a computer and a reliable veterinary nurse.'

'Grace has never worked a computer,' Elissa murmured uncertainly. 'She was the only other person my father had to help him, apart from myself when I was home.'

Adam shrugged. 'Not to worry. Technology is relatively easy to understand once the fundamentals are learned. I think we should invest straight away in desktop equipment for here in the office and Reception.'

Elissa found it hard to explain how she was feeling, even to herself. All she knew was that suddenly this man had come into her life and it was being turned upside down. Though she knew change was important and unavoidable, she felt deep resentment at his manner.

'What kind of ophthalmic equipment have you in storage?' Elissa asked, trying to steer the conversation in a different direction.

'I've invested in a brand-new ophthalmic microscope. Using one abroad, I just couldn't imagine working without one now. The trouble is, it needs a theatre to itself, as you probably know.' He paused and she waited apprehensively, as he gave her an uncertain frown. 'As a matter of fact I wondered — and this is merely a suggestion of course — if I could install it in the smaller of the two theatres for the time being. The larger one will take two tables easily, which we could use for general surgery. This would mean I could begin to take referral clients immediately.'

Elissa felt inexplicably stricken. On the whole it sounded a reasonable suggestion, but deep down she felt a bewildering reluctance to effect such a change.

'Of course, if you would prefer we wait . . . ' her companion murmured, aware of her silence.

Elissa shrugged. 'I suppose . . . We rarely used the smaller theatre . . . '

Adam frowned, briefly casting his dark eyes over her face. 'You don't sound too sure?'

She wasn't sure, that was true. Her apprehension was impossible to explain, since his suggestion seemed perfectly justified. 'We can certainly see how it works,' Elissa compromised, her tone cool. She glanced at her watch. 'Is there anything else of importance we should discuss today?'

He paused, then said thoughtfully, 'Have you any suggestions as to who you would like to do the redecorative work?'

She tried to focus her thoughts, to drag them back from the question of the theatre conversion. 'Dad employed a handyman in Farwell. Perhaps he might be able to help.'

'I've the number of a professional firm in Shrewsbury,' he suggested swiftly. 'The firm comes by way of recommendation from a friend of mine. I'll make some enquiries, if you've no objection?'

Elissa shrugged. 'Yes, all right.' She moved towards the door. 'If you don't need me any more — '

He held out a hand as he began to dial the number. 'Don't go just yet. I may be able to sort something out for Monday.'

Soon he was deep in conversation and Elissa sighed, walking to reception as he made the call, feeling that her new partner had something of an aura of a typhoon about him, a whirlwind of energy whipping in the atmosphere.

How long, for instance, had he been thinking the theatre conversion over? And furthermore, should she have agreed to it? The question really was, she reflected soberly, that when the large theatre with two tables was adequate for both of them to operate if needs be, what grounds did she have for disagreeing?

When Adam emerged, he looked triumphant. 'They're sending someone tomorrow afternoon with colour-charts and samples. It's Sunday, but I impressed on them the urgency, and the manager himself said he would call. With luck, he may be able to provide a team for Monday to begin the preparatory work.'

'Monday!' Elissa gasped in surprise.

His black brows signalled amusement. 'Don't leave until tomorrow what can be done today. And that reminds me, I've a few ideas I'd like to run through with you on special healthcare projects.'

Her heart started to race. 'This is my afternoon off, Adam,' she said, with a look of alarm on her face. 'We shall have plenty of time for discussion tomorrow.'

He caught her arm as she moved. 'Elissa, I know you have doubts and I don't want to rush you. But Larkhill deserves a new image; we owe it to ourselves and our partnership. I have the utmost respect for your father's work. But this is a new and fast-moving decade. Only with the most up-to-date equipment and in the freshest of surroundings can you and I work to the best of our potential.'

'You've made your point quite clear,' she retorted crisply. 'You will have to excuse me, for, though you may have eaten lunch, I haven't.' She paused by the door. 'If you really do need me, I'll be in my flat for the rest of the afternoon.'

It was easy for Adam Kennedy to alter a person's lifestyle without so much as a second thought, Elissa reflected miserably that evening as she fell tiredly into bed. He might be happy with instant change taking place in a house which had not been his home, but she had lived at Larkhill all her life.

Or was it she who was deceiving herself? she wondered as she drifted into sleep. Was her head telling her Adam's refurbishment and expansion suggestions were perfectly justified, while her heart was resenting them deeply?

These were her last thoughts as she

drifted into uneasy sleep, wondering if, above her, the new resident was mentally turning the rooms upside down and painting them from top to toe.

★ ★ ★

Early on Sunday, Elissa showered and dressed in white shorts and lemon tie-waist shirt. She made coffee in the kitchen and fed Jemima, who slithered in through the cat-flap, pressing her wet blue nose against Elissa's ankle. Then she went through the connecting door to the surgery to feed Trinka and Honeybunch, but halfway along the passage she sensed someone already in the surgery.

She pushed open the office door. Adam sat at her father's desk, his dark head bent over a pile of papers.

'Good morning! I thought I'd just go through a few invoices.' He smiled pleasantly as he looked up at her. 'I didn't want to disturb you.'

Elissa tried to shrug off her irritation. It was irrational, she knew, to resent his sitting there, going through her father's paperwork. He was obviously entitled to, but all the same, it was disconcerting.

'Did you have a comfortable night?' she asked, trying to compose herself.

'Extremely. I feel quite at home.'

'I wondered if you managed to find your way around the kitchen this morning?'

He smiled, stretching his long brown arms above his head. 'No problem. I remembered to do a little shopping yesterday so I've left all my groceries on the worktop for Grace to dispatch.'

Elissa frowned at the papers he was studying. 'Can I help?'

'Not really. I was just making myself familiar with the position as it stands. I did wonder why your father was called in to treat Honeybunch and Trinka, though. Surely the wildlife park has its own vet?'

Elissa nodded. 'Yes, they do. But Dad

was well-known for his interest in wild animals.' She smiled reflectively. 'When one of the keepers told him of the little orphan's plight and no immediate surrogate mother could be found, he offered his help.'

'He must have been a very dedicated man,' Adam murmured softly.

Dedication was the word, Elissa thought, remembering the hours her father had spent in rearing Honeybunch and making up the special pens with the run leading out into the garden. 'As for Trinka,' she sighed distractedly, 'Dad suggested the problem with her was simply behavioural — attention-seeking. The wildlife park were going to transfer her until Dad suggested all she needed was her teeth levelling and the problem would be solved, in so far as she would realise she couldn't gain attention by biting. It was a bit of a gamble . . . '

'Which paid off.'

Elissa's green eyes softened. 'Unfortunately he was never able to do the work himself, as you know. I only wish he were alive to see how Trinka has improved.'

'Fortunately, he had a daughter who could complete his work for him,' Adam reminded her gently.

Elissa stiffened. She didn't want to talk any more about her father; the memories were still too painful, often accompanied by emotions she couldn't yet be sure of controlling.

'Is there anything else?' she asked briskly, and moved automatically towards the door.

He shook his head, getting up. 'Look, I'll disappear for a few hours and get out from under your feet.'

When he was gone, she wished she had not been so brusque. She had been trying to convince herself that the resentment she felt against Adam wouldn't last, or maybe she could just ignore it. And yet her irritation was mixed with something else which she couldn't ignore. He made her feel vulnerable, as though he could look right inside her, even see what she was thinking . . . as he had just then, when he obviously decided it was better to leave her to her own devices.

★   ★   ★

A tall, well-dressed businessman arrived after lunch and pushed the bell on the house door. 'Mr Kennedy? Miss Hart?' he asked with a bright smile. 'I'm Mr Rumble from Bensons in Shrewsbury.'

Together all three went into the surgery, where the man sighed reprovingly as he looked round. 'Oh, yes, rather a lot of work to be done, I see!'

Adam grinned at Elissa. 'We've a fair idea of what we would like. Elissa, do you want to begin?'

She nodded as her eye caught a delicious shade of very pale lemon highlighted in one of the books. 'That's beautiful. I'd like this shade for my consulting-room.'

Mr Rumble nodded. 'Excellent choice. We have blinds and drapes of the same shade.'

They continued to sift through the

catalogues, deciding on pastels for the treatment-rooms and white throughout in the theatres and reception-rooms. Mr Rumble suggested small details, like elegant little golden door-knobs here and there, and some durable, easy-cleaning floor covering.

'We should have new washbasins,' Elissa added, remembering that the one in her room leaked.

'Ah,' sighed Mr Rumble delightedly, 'our plumbing department's speciality. Have a look at these.'

There was, Elissa realised, nothing that Mr Rumble could not produce from his briefcase.

'Well? What do you think?' Adam grinned, as they stood in the sunshine several hours later, with a promise of decorators to begin first thing in the morning. 'That wasn't too painful, was it? All there is left to do is submit the order for our new equipment tomorrow morning. Most of it should be here later this week.'

'I'm surprised Bensons could begin

so quickly,' Elissa confessed. 'I was almost expecting Mr Rumble to produce a white rabbit from that fat briefcase of his!'

Adam laughed. 'Yes, he is rather spectacular. My colleague, Peter Sharp, was right about his efficiency.'

Elissa frowned. 'Peter Sharp . . . This your friend who lives in Shropshire?'

Adam nodded. 'Peter and I trained together. He went into orthopaedics, but we never lost contact. Actually, it was while I was staying with them after I came back from the States that I read your advertisement. A stroke of luck, as a matter of fact.'

Luck certainly seemed to be on Adam's side, Elissa reflected, as she discovered him the following morning helping Grace in the kitchen, and wondered what stroke of luck had brought him into Grace's good books as he helped her with the breakfast.

He turned and smiled as he spooned two brown farm eggs into egg-cups straight from the boiling water. 'Exactly three minutes. Lightly boiled is how you like them, so I gather?'

'Morning, Elissa,' Grace called as she poured coffee. 'Yes, we've had a long chat, Adam and I. Now sit down and eat your breakfast.'

Adam pulled out two chairs. He skimmed off the top of his egg with a flourish. 'Actually, Grace and I have been discussing a few things. For instance, in the past, I understand, she went in to help your father at about eleven, isn't that right, Grace?'

'Eleven or twelve, depending on how urgently he needed me,' she agreed.

Adam hesitated, frowning at Elissa. 'Well ... As we grow busier, Grace won't be able to divide herself in two looking after us and coming in to assist in surgery. I suggest we employ a nurse — or maybe two — which will leave Grace free to concentrate on the house. What do you think?'

Grace interrupted. 'It does seem at my age — I'm fifty-four, Elissa — it would be far better for you to get someone younger who you could train.'

Elissa stared at Grace in astonishment, but the older woman merely smiled and said swiftly, 'I'm happy to help in the house still, Elissa. There's plenty to occupy me here.'

Elissa noticed that Adam continued to chew on his toast as though he hadn't a care in the world.

She scraped back her chair and stood up angrily. 'Well, it does seem it's all arranged. If you're happy with that arrangement, Grace?' She glared at Adam. 'If you'll excuse me, I have a practice to open!'

Trinka snorted with delight as, to distract herself from her anger, Elissa prepared a healthy mixture of scrambled eggs and fruit for the little chimpanzee. With her teeth planed down, Trinka had realised that she no longer had the power to inflict damage and, as Elissa opened her cage, Trinka strung her long arms around her neck and pushed out her fat lips.

'Yes, I love you too,' Elissa whispered, savouring the cuddle and trying not to think about what had just taken place in the kitchen.

From Reception Elissa heard sounds of what could only be the army of Mr Rumble's Monday-morning decorators. Well, Adam could deal with them! But all too soon she heard his voice in the corridor coming her way.

'Do I get a cuddle too?' he asked cheerfully as he walked in.

Trinka shrieked and, in feckless mood, held out her arms to him. He took her gently, smiling down at Elissa as the monkey wrapped herself around his neck. 'Did I say something to upset you, back there in the kitchen?' he asked hesitantly.

Elissa felt angry adrenalin throb in her veins. 'How could you do that to Grace — and without consulting me first!'

He shook his head, frowning deeply. 'I'm sorry, I'm not with you . . . What have I done to Grace?'

'You know very well, Adam!' Elissa turned deliberately away to lower to a yawning Honeybunch his minced meat.

'Stop being so busy for a minute, Elissa,' Adam commanded, placing the chimp back beside her breakfast and closing the door of the cage. 'Come into my room. I want to talk to you.' He took hold of her arm and propelled her along the passageway. Closing the door with a thud behind them, he frowned angrily at her. 'What exactly have I done wrong?'

'Surely it's obvious?' Elissa tried in vain to control the sweep of colour into her cheeks.

'It's obvious you're upset, yes!' he observed thickly.

'Of course I'm upset. Grace has been with my father for years. She was a friend of my mother's — she's part of the family! I couldn't have managed without her support over the last weeks and Dad would have done anything — anything at all — to keep her as a nurse! She may be getting a little older and slower and she might not be as nimble as she was once was, but that's absolutely no reason at all to tell her she's unsuitable for the practice — '

'I didn't,' he interrupted coolly.

'But I heard you!' Her voice was shaking.

'You heard what you wanted to hear.'

'You convinced Grace she was . . . obsolete!' Elissa hurled fiercely.

He matched her resentful green stare with angry dark eyes. 'I did nothing of the kind. Grace wanted to give up nursing of her own accord.'

'But that can't be true!' Elissa gasped disbelievingly. 'She would never give up something so dear to her!'

'I'm afraid she has to.' Adam's tone was bleak. 'The work takes too much from her at her age. Her loyalty to your father was unquestionable, but shortly before he died, Grace began to feel unwell. Her blood-pressure is far too high and her doctor advised her to take things more easily. Unfortunately she was so conscientious she couldn't bring herself to speak up.'

'But . . . but why didn't she tell me?'

Elissa forced back the hurt from her eyes.

Adam reached out, gently touching her shoulder. 'Because you've been grieving, and Grace felt one more blow would be particularly unkind.'

Elissa swallowed on the lump in her throat. 'Grace told you that?'

He nodded, his fingers slipping away. 'I should have encouraged Grace to talk to you herself. My suggestion on her behalf back-fired, I'm afraid.'

Elissa groaned miserably. 'I've been too preoccupied to notice she hasn't been well. Poor Grace.' She looked up at him, suddenly seeing the situation in its true perspective. 'I thought you . . .'

'You thought quite wrongly, Elissa.' He stiffened, his dark eyes hurt. 'I'm sorry you have such a low opinion of me.'

Blushing deeply, she was ashamed of her impetuous reaction. But before she could apologise, one of the decorators hurried into the room. 'You've got some customers lining up out here. I'm just trying to keep them out of my emulsion-pots!'

Adam's dark eyebrows shot up. With a rueful smile he tilted his head. 'Coming?'

Elissa suddenly wished she'd got up at the crack of dawn. 'I haven't even begun to clear up in here!'

'Leave it for now,' he called, already on his way down the corridor. 'I'll help you later.'

Amid the turmoil, Elissa gasped at the array of clients perched on whatever available seating they could find in between ladders and paint-pots. Some she recognised. Others were completely new to her. But they were all women — and they were all looking admiringly at the man who stood beside her. Obviously the word about Farwell's handsome new vet had circulated on the grape-vine, Elissa realised, as Adam began introducing himself.

In the stream of booster vaccinations, interspersed with answering curious questions on Larkhill's new partner,

Elissa also took some encouraging appointments for the rest of the week. Fortunately, the decorators went calmly about their business. Somehow the afternoon progressed without one spilt pot or lead entwined in a ladder.

Just before closing, Elissa walked into the empty reception area, devoid now of decorators, to discover an older man breathlessly standing in the doorway. He looked so ill that she hurried to his side and helped him to a chair.

'Thank you,' he gasped wheezily. 'I've walked rather too far.' He glanced down at a large brindled wolfhound which had sunk to the floor beside him. 'And so has Arnold.'

Adam appeared, saying goodbye to his last client. 'Is anything wrong?' he asked, frowning in concern and coming over.

'I . . . I'm afraid it's my heart condition,' explained the man. 'I'm due to go in for a by-pass soon. I thought I could manage the short walk here, but I'm afraid it's taken all my strength. And Arnie's too. I'm afraid he's not a lot better in health than I am.'

Elissa hurried to fetch a glass of water. When he had sipped from it, he looked up gratefully. 'Arnold is out of breath,' he sighed, looking down at the panting dog. 'If I didn't know better, I would say he's coming out in sympathy with me.'

Adam nodded. 'We'll take a look at him, but it would be better if you could come into a consulting-room. Do you think you can manage the walk if we give you some assistance?' Very slowly, they managed the corridor, and soon the dog's owner was seated on a comfortable chair in Adam's room.

Mr Martin sighed as Adam examined the dog. 'He's as tired as I am. Doesn't want to walk, and sleeps all the time. He's six, but you'd think he was a hundred and six. You'd never believe the children next door called him Arnie because he's always been so big and strong.'

Arnold lifted dull browny-grey eyes towards Elissa as Adam slipped his stethoscope over the dog's chest to listen to his heartbeat.

'I'm afraid I have a distinct pulse irregularity,' Adam sighed in dismay. He passed the stethoscope to her and she listened carefully, hearing at once the distortion of the aortic murmur. But telling the old man bad news would surely only worsen the situation, and Elissa knew by Adam's reticence that the same thought had occurred to him too.

'The positive side is,' Adam began with a reassuring smile, 'I can find no obvious pulmonary congestion. Heart muscle disease often affects large breeds, and at Arnie's age he will have to be given assistance with some form of medication. However, we shan't know more until we do further tests.'

'But I can't afford very expensive treatment!'

Adam nodded. 'Let's take each step at a time and see how we get along with the tests first.'

Mr Martin looked up in surprise.

'But what if it's serious? What will happen to him while I'm in hospital — who will look after him? If he's ill, how can I ask anyone to take the responsibility of looking after a sick dog?'

Elissa thought of what her father would have done. He would have treated and boarded the dog and considered costs later, though, in retrospect, she had to admit that this kind of generosity was probably what had landed him in such financial disaster. She could hardly expect Adam to follow suit.

Adam bent to stroke Arnie thoughtfully. 'Well . . . We could board him here. The expenses would be minimal, I'm sure,' he suggested, and Elissa stared at him in surprise.

Mr Martin was silent for a moment. Then he said softly, 'That's very kind of you. I just don't know what to say.'

Adam trailed his hand over the animal's grey head. 'Arnold may fret a little at first, but Elissa and I would take care of him until you're recovered, wouldn't we, Elissa? Neither of us has a dog, so he'd get lots of attention.'

She nodded, staring at him under her lashes, hardly able to believe that he had made the suggestion.

At length Adam slipped off his white coat to replace it with a sports jacket and, helping Mr Martin to his feet, led him to the Mercedes to drive him home, leaving Arnie in Elissa's care.

She sat quietly with the dog, her mind reviewing the events of the day. More than ever she regretted her suspicions of Adam regarding Grace and, after the way he had handled the problem of Mr Martin and Arnie, she was forced to admit that he had behaved most generously.

Then why, she wondered, did she feel so confused? As Jemima poked her blue nose into the consulting-room, a fringe of hair stood up on her back as though she were electrified at the sight of Arnie. She hissed and wrinkled her stubby nose, her bushy blue tail ramrod-straight.

Arnie made no attempt to retaliate, but snuffled his beard into Elissa's ankles with a deep sigh.

'Gentle giant, aren't you Arnold?' she whispered lovingly, reflecting wryly that Jemima's reaction to Arnie was all too reminiscent of the way she herself had behaved towards Adam Kennedy.

3

The following morning Harry Fitzroy pulled up in his beige Range Rover. He gave his usual toot on the horn, just managed to park in between the decorators' vans, and climbed out. Elissa opened Larkhill's front door to a bright July day, waving at him as he strode across the drive.

'How lovely to see you!' She welcomed her godfather with a fond embrace, and he returned it with a cheerful hug, raising bushy grey eyebrows at the activity of the decorators. Her godfather had moved with the times and expanded over the years to three successful practices dotted over the county. Harry and her father had been friends since they both set up their plates in the sixties, and it was Harry who had called her in France and broken the news of her father's coronary.

Elissa remembered gratefully his generous offer to clear her father's debts, even suggesting she merge Larkhill with his own practice. Her idea of finding a partner had been met with concern, though she knew it was genuine concern for her sake. She wondered what Harry would make of Adam and if, this morning, he had called to see for himself.

'My goodness, what a hive of activity!' he grinned, grey eyebrows shooting up.

She smiled ruefully. 'My new practice partner managed to get heaven and earth moving the moment he moved in!'

'All's well, hopefully?' Harry enquired tactfully, studying her face. She had told him about Adam Kennedy over the phone, but she could see he was curious.

Elissa threaded her hand through the arm of the old tweed jacket. 'Come and see for yourself. I'll introduce you.'

They discovered Adam in the surgery garden, where he was leaning over Honeybunch's pen, watching the cub play with Jemima.

Elissa felt a start as she stared at the little scene. Adam must have risen early to clean the pens; his brown arms were naked in the sunshine, shirt-sleeves rolled across the strong muscles.

'Good morning!' he called as he saw them, his dark eyes warm under the shock of black hair.

Introductions were made, and soon the men were talking animatedly. Elissa distracted herself by going into the pen. There was little to do, for even the lion cub-sized cat-flap into the recovery-room was as clean as a whistle and the concrete hosed down, with a fresh smell of disinfectant everywhere.

She stacked a bale of straw on its end and pulled some out for Honeybunch to play in. Out of the corner of her eye she watched Adam, noticing the easy way he stood and talked to Harry, with his long muscled legs under the jeans complementing his height and broad shoulders.

What was it about him, she wondered, that really disturbed her? Something in his dark, male expression perhaps, that made her heart pound faster. But recovering herself quickly, she realised that Harry was calling, and went over.

'Honeybunch is looking marvellous, now,' he said in genuine admiration of the cub. 'You'll soon have him ready for the wildlife park, won't you?'

Elissa let herself out of the pen. 'Yes, it's hard to think three months ago he could have died,' she murmured with a sigh. 'He's fully weaned now — but he still loves his milk, especially his old bottle.'

'If I know anything about women, you won't want to see him go,' Harry smiled ruefully.

Her colour rose as she tried to avoid the men's eyes, sweeping her gaze down to Honeybunch, who lumbered clumsily towards Jemima and fell over before he could pounce on her. His coat was thick and soft and smelt of the wild, reminding her of Africa. His teeth were sharp, his growl impressive. But he always retracted his claws when she played with him, as he did with Jemima.

Jemima miaowed, jumped on Honey-bunch's back and began to knead her claws into his thick coat. Showing a remarkable degree of tolerance, Honey-bunch took a swipe at her with innocent malice.

Everyone laughed. 'He still thinks of Jemima as his mother,' Elissa grinned. 'He models himself on her, using his paws like hers.'

'Considering his size, three times Jemima's, it can't do much for his ego,' observed Adam wryly. 'I think Harry's right. We should be getting him back with other cubs if the wildlife park have any.'

Elissa resisted. 'All in good time. I want to make sure he digests his minced beef and tripe properly. We've come this far, and Dad wouldn't want any mistakes.'

An uneasy silence descended, before Harry cleared his throat and patted his pockets. 'Well, Adam, very glad to have met you. It'll be handy to be able to refer all my difficult ophthalmic cases to you. You'll be in full swing soon, I take it?'

'Next week, with luck.' Adam glanced at Elissa. 'The decorators are pretty swift . . . Our new equipment arrives Friday . . . Yes, next week, with luck.'

Harry shook his hand warmly and her godfather bent to kiss her cheek. As they accompanied him to his Range Rover, he laughed aloud, shaking his head. 'Nearly forgot what I came for! Are you thinking of taking on a veterinary nurse or two, as you've begun in earnest?'

Adam shrugged his broad shoulders as he stood next to Elissa, taking care not to meet her gaze. He nodded. 'Yes, actually we've been thinking of advertising.'

'Don't bother,' Harry said, surprisingly. 'I advertised myself last week. Had a good response, but I only wanted one nurse to replace someone who'd left. Pity, because all the applicants were darn nice girls. I've a list of those who applied. Would you be interested?'

Adam glanced at Elissa. She hesitated, then finally nodded, for she knew that sooner or later they must have help and probably sooner was better.

'Thanks a lot,' Adam called, as Harry climbed into the Range Rover and the engine choked into life.

'I'll be in touch.' Harry hesitated before reversing. 'And don't forget, any time you need to have your calls diverted through to my practice, we'll cover for you. Just give us a few hours' notice if you can. You'll find it hard going just between the two of you at first.'

When they were alone and walking back to the practice, Adam asked, 'Was that OK with you?'

'Regarding the VNs?' Elissa shrugged. 'Yes, of course.'

'I like Harry,' Adam said as they went. 'And it's very useful to be able to count on his help with calls should the need arise.'

Elissa nodded. 'He always helped

Dad out. They were very close.' She hadn't meant that to sound quite so cutting, though, as she glanced at Adam's face, she knew the inference had gone home, for his mouth tightened into a straight line and he pushed his hands deeply into his pockets as they walked.

'I'm just going to check I closed the pen securely,' Elissa said suddenly as they reached the practice. For some reason she felt the need to distance herself from him before she began work. A few minutes' fresh air might clear her head and the uncomfortable little ache that played around her ribs.

'I'll come with you,' he said, to her dismay.

They walked around by the side entrance in silence. Sun filled the garden and deepened the colours of the trees. It was so beautifully tranquil that Elissa stopped for a second by the French windows which led into her apartment. Sharp arrows of light glinted off the glass and caused her to shade her eyes.

'Just a minute.' Adam frowned. 'Don't move, you've some straw in your hair. Let me take it out for you.' He reached up, gently untangling the straw from her thick hair, his fingers soft and agile, separating the red-brown waves to ease out the slivers.

'All done,' he smiled, staring down at her. Then, hesitantly, he said, 'You've lovely hair. Such a beautiful rich colour. It reminds me of a squirrel's coat, the red ones you hardly ever see these days.'

She tried to step away but she found she couldn't. All she could do was stare into those dark eyes. Suddenly he drew the knuckles of his fingers down the curve of her cheek, pushing back the hair from her face.

He smoothed her cheek again, causing her to tremble lightly, her breath held in suspense. Both his hands came up to cup her face. 'Elissa . . .'

A shimmering sensation ran under her skin where his fingers touched her, and she waited for him to speak, to say more, but he remained silent, just holding her face lightly in the sunshine, his eyes locked intensely on her lips.

Then, as he gently brought his lips to hers, she felt herself move unresistingly on to tiptoe and her mouth curved open involuntarily as the warmth of his body permeated through to her.

Almost without her knowing it, her hands slipped to his shoulders. Her fingers went up to his thick dark hair and her body began to burn. She closed her eyes, allowing the sensation to sweep over her, and suddenly the kiss was no longer gentle and uncertain, but his hands came to the small of her back to pull her closer, his mouth beginning to cover hers in deep, exploratory possession.

His hair felt crisp and clean to her touch. Raw sensations of desire ran through her as her fingers wound themseves in the thickness. Her heart thudded as she dimly tried to convince herself that this wasn't happening and she wasn't returning the kiss of a man for whom she had felt such dislike only a few moments ago.

The shudder of her body, she knew, was what caused him to pull away. As she stared up at him, her lips burning, a slight semblance of sanity returned and she flattened her hands against his chest.

Gently brushing back her hair, he refused to let her go. 'I couldn't resist doing that, I'm afraid. I was watching you in Honeybunch's pen, dressed in those khaki shorts and your African T-shirt and the cub rolling at your feet . . . '

Suddenly the mention of Africa seemed to bring everything clearly into focus. Africa, then France and then . . . The picture of her father, as she had last seen him before she went, was suddenly achingly bright in her mind.

'Elissa?' He frowned deeply as she pulled out of his arms.

'I . . . That is . . . ' she began, her voice seeming faint, 'we're putting our professional partnership at risk . . . We shouldn't have done that.'

'I wasn't thinking of our professional relationship when I kissed you,' he murmured, coming to stand beside her. 'In fact I wasn't thinking of anything except how very much I wanted to take you in my arms.'

She tensed, drawing away, frightened by her own emotions. To her relief she heard the barking of dogs coming from the drive. 'We have clients arriving,' she said shakily.

'I don't want to leave things like this,' Adam muttered, grabbing her arm as she moved away. 'We should talk, Elissa.'

She was silent again. 'There's really nothing to talk about,' she said finally, as she looked up at him. 'Sometimes things go out of control and it's no one's fault. So let's forget about the last few minutes ... As far as I'm concerned, Adam, it never happened.'

He stared at her, searching her face with questioning eyes. 'If that's what you want?'

There was a momentary silence, and Elissa nodded. 'I think we'd better go.'

They walked without a word to the front of the house. A hatchback had arrived, and two red setters barked excitedly as the owner struggled to attach them to leads.

'You go ahead and change,' Adam said coolly. 'I'll tell them we shan't be very long.'

In her bedroom Elissa slipped off her shorts and put on a blue summer blouse and skirt, her fingers trembling over the cloth. She stared, flushed and confused, at her reflection in the mirror, at the place on her lips where he had kissed her.

She'd never had time to think about her looks very much. Animals had always come first. Her desire to be a vet. To cure. To care. No man had ever kissed her the way Adam Kennedy had kissed her today. She'd never felt like that in her life before.

Whatever was wrong with her? she wondered, making an effort to compose herself. Brushing her long red hair until it shone in waves, she tried to put the incident out of her mind as a small setback in their relationship. After all, it was just a kiss and they had both decided to ignore the fact that it had ever happened.

★ ★ ★

Since Adam was seeing the two setters for boosters, Elissa saw the next patient to arrive, a Cavalier King Charles. It took an effort to concentrate, but she told herself she must.

The Cavalier showed signs of a 'wet face', typical of this kind of breed: wetness under the eyes, staining the white fur a dirty brown.

Elissa examined the eye with her pen torch. As neither eye seemed painful, but was distressful more to the owner than the dog, Elissa tried to explain that the nasal drainage of tears was very much the norm for a dog of this type.

'The cornea is healthy,' Elissa remarked,

swabbing the area as the well-behaved dog sat still and allowed her to proceed. 'But I'm going to put in these drops, which will take about fifteen minutes to work.'

'What will they do?' enquired the woman doubtfully, as Elissa administered the drops.

'I shall be able to have a full view of the lens, very much like the optician would put optical fluid into a human eye so he can see it in finer detail.'

Considering the matter, Elissa added, 'If you'd like to sit down by him, I'll just see who else we have waiting.'

Though Elissa intended to look into Reception, first she went into the office and buzzed through to Adam on the intercom.

'Adam, I'm sorry to disturb you, but I have a Cavalier King Charles with a wet face. He doesn't appear to be in any discomfort but I'd like you to make sure there's no deep-seated problem. Would you like my first referral?'

'Of course. Please book the dog in.

Perhaps make an appointment for a week's time?' He hesitated. 'Elissa?'

'Yes?'

'Am I forgiven?'

'What's to forgive?' she asked lightly, wishing she felt as careless as she sounded.

But as she went back to her room, she kept remembering the way his mouth had felt over hers, and colour burned in her cheeks wildly. She felt confused and unsettled. Maybe her natural pride was hurt, having to accept Adam's help with the practice. Perhaps sharing was the root of the trouble; for years before, she had shared Larkhill only with her father. And yet the way she had physically responded to Adam today had shaken her. He had taken her into his arms and she had done nothing to resist his kiss.

Discovering no obvious sign of lens infection or damage to the Cavalier's eye, Elissa prescribed some soothing drops and made an appointment for a week's time, hoping that by then the small theatre would be transformed into the unit.

The day progressed with a few minor ailments, and at half-past three there was a call from a farmer, an acquaintance of her father's who had heard that Larkhill was active once more.

Elissa had no more clients, and she went in to tell Adam she was making the call. However, when she went out to her car, the old vehicle spluttered and choked and flatly refused to start.

Adam came out and gestured to the bonnet. 'I'll have a quick look for you. Release the bonnet catch.'

He was lost from sight for the next five minutes. When he emerged he shook his head. 'Bad news, I'm afraid. The head gasket's gone. I'm sorry, but I really do think this engine has seen better days.'

'Just when I needed transport,' Elissa sighed, wondering what on earth she was going to do about the call to the farm.

'Take mine,' he suggested. 'I'm insured

for a named driver. It's a straight-forward gearbox, you'll have no trouble in driving it.'

'Are you sure?' Elissa stared doubt-fully at the sleek Mercedes.

'Here are the keys.' He wiped his hands on a rag and dug into his pock-ets, pushing the keys into her palm. 'Don't forget your case.'

Elissa hesitated, but Adam tugged her case from her car and bundled her into the Mercedes.

'She'll drive herself,' he assured her, leaning in at the window, and she caught the drift of his aftershave. At once she stalled the engine. Then she tried again and, under his amused glance, the engine purred like a satisfied cat.

Soon she was on her way, watching Adam's tall figure in the mirror disap-pearing from view.

★　★　★

Elissa welcomed getting back to treat-ing large animals. In Africa she'd had the opportunity to indulge her passion for them, some as spectacular as reserve elephants whose tusks had been damaged by poachers.

Examining an animal not quite so unusual at White Farm, a brown and white Ayrshire cow, Elissa donned gloves and protective clothing.

'You aren't sure if she's pregnant?' she asked, lifting the cow's tail.

'She's disappointed me before,' Sam Lowe sighed. 'Like to get a nice calf from her, but she hasn't taken in the past. That's why I wanted to be sure. Second only to Frisians, you know, for milk yield, are these Ayrshires.'

Elissa entered the cow and, by palpation of the cow's womb through the wall of the rectum, she diagnosed her to be rather more than two months in duration. She thought how many times her father had confirmed pregnancies like this; and how many times he had 'forgotten' to make a note of a call, if the farmer or smallholder had problems or was running into trouble under the harsh restraints of the economic climate.

'Yes, I can confirm her pregnancy, Sam,' Elissa said at last. 'You should get your calf. She's certainly two months gone.'

The farmer gave a satisfied sigh. Then he asked with a curious frown, 'How's that new man of yours coming along?'

'Oh . . . Adam?' Elissa hesitated as she washed her hands and arms in the warm water provided. 'He's settling in, I think.'

'Know anything about beasts, does he, or just toys on leads?'

Elissa laughed, her green eyes twinkling. 'Oh, yes, Sam, he knows about animals. In fact he's a specialist in his own field, ophthalmology.'

The old farmer frowned. 'You mean eyes!'

Elissa slipped her examination gown off, freeing her hair from the band so that it spilled around her shoulders. Then she stepped out of her boots and back into her summer sandals.

'He'll have his work cut out all right,' smiled Sam as he walked her to the barn door.

'You mean in getting to know people? Oh, I don't think it will take him too long to become acclimatised. He's already extremely popular with the clients.'

'No, I didn't mean the clients!' Sam handed over her case, chuckling. 'I mean nearer to home. You haven't got that colour hair for nothing and I should know. The wife's going grey now, but when she was younger she was the same!' Sam flinched at the memory, and Elissa couldn't help laughing too.

'Bit of a posh car, isn't it, for a little thing like you?' Sam observed as she climbed in and started the engine.

'Just on loan I'm afraid, Sam. Dad's old car has given up the ghost.'

'Get yourself something sturdy,' the farmer advised. 'Like my old girl there. Ideal for rough roads.'

Elissa glanced at the muddy green Land Rover and her heart gave a little jerk. On the way home, she thought of the second vehicle her father had kept locked away in the garage. Just as she was turning it over in her mind, Larkhill came into view and she slid the Mercedes to a halt.

It was a surprise to find Adam in the office. Seated in the chair behind the desk with Arnie at his feet, he had made coffee in mugs for himself and his companion. A pretty young blonde woman looked slightly flushed as Elissa walked in.

'Elissa, this is Miss Fielding.'

'Sharon, please,' interrupted the girl, who held out her hand and shook Elissa's. She had clear bright blue eyes and a friendly smile.

'Harry rang Sharon to say we were looking for a VN,' Adam explained.

'And I came immediately,' the young woman added. 'Mr Fitzroy had already chosen an applicant for his vacant situation. But he kindly kept my number, just in case.'

Elissa smiled and sat down on the

spare chair. 'Has Adam shown you over the practice?'

Sharon Fielding nodded. 'And I've met Trinka and Honeybunch — and Arnie, of course.'

'You live locally, Sharon?'

'With my sister for the time being. I'm originally from York, where I trained with a vet after leaving school. I passed my preliminary and finals with the practice and stayed for four years. I left because I really feel I could do with a change and, having stayed with Anne and her husband for holidays, I think I'd like to settle here in Shropshire. It's such a beautiful county.'

'Were you at an all-rounder practice?' Adam enquired.

'Yes, farms and small animals. Mr Deacon, the senior partner of six vets, has given me references.'

'A big practice. You must have been very busy.' Elissa raised her eyebrows, impressed.

Sharon nodded. 'Very busy. But as the practice grew it seemed to lose a little of the personal touch. Mr Fitzroy told me Larkhill was just starting up again — he explained your father had died, Miss Hart. I'm extremely sorry.' She hesitated, adding quickly, 'That's why I came over now. I didn't want to miss another opportunity.'

Elissa smiled. 'It's nice to see such enthusiasm.' She explained briefly what was going on with the refurbishment and Adam's plans for the referral unit.

'Arnold is our first patient and we've got him in for observation,' Adam said, as Sharon bent down and ran her hand over his thick coat. 'We're looking for someone whose love of animals is of course the priority, plus patience and a calm manner . . . and someone who is in very good health and can stand up to a long day.'

Sharon nodded. 'We worked shifts in York. There were four of us, but two were trainees. I'm quite used to long hours and night-shifts and organising the shifts and rotas. I'm also familiar with Theatre work, which is actually my favourite. But I've acted as receptionist and office clerk — ' she laughed lightly ' — and of course, cleaning out is second nature, that goes without saying. One thing in a large practice, you do almost every job under the sun.'

Elissa realised that neither she nor Adam had talked about the terms and conditions of employment. The same thing must have been on Adam's mind, for he ran a large hand over his chin and asked the girl what she had been accustomed to.

'It seems very fair to me,' Adam sighed at length, and Elissa nodded. 'I think we could match that.'

Arnie laid his head in Sharon's lap. 'It seems you've made a friend in Arnie already,' Adam grinned. Sharon laughed and cuddled the dog, but suddenly she frowned.

'He's very lethargic, isn't he?' She glanced at Adam. 'We had several large dogs with heart complaints who looked a bit like Arnie. Has he had an ECG?'

Adam nodded. 'I ran some tests

through this afternoon. Poor results at the moment, I'm afraid. As soon as our new ultrasound arrives I'll scan him, but we suspect cardiopathy.' Turning to Elissa, he said, 'I've started him on digoxin. So we'll see how he goes.'

Elissa nodded. It was impressive that Sharon had picked up his condition and she knew that Adam must be aware of it too.

Adam said, 'We will probably need another veterinary nurse, but as yet we haven't had time to advertise.'

'Oh,' the young woman sighed disappointedly. 'I understand. You'd like to interview everyone before making a decision.'

Elissa glanced briefly at Adam. 'Not at all. If you would like to think about the job, then fine, but it's yours if you want it.'

'Really?' gasped Sharon. 'Oh, no, I don't need to think about it at all. I'd like to accept, thank you.'

'When would you be able to start?' Elissa asked.

Sharon's reply came without hesitation. 'Now, if you want me!'

Everyone laughed. Even Arnie managed to wag his tail and duck his head under Sharon's hand for another stroke.

'Well, what do you think?' Adam asked when they were alone.

'I think we're very fortunate to have found her,' Elissa said without hesitation.

'Good. One problem solved. Now for the next. Your car.'

'Oh dear, yes.' Elissa looked up at him gratefully. 'Thank you for the loan of the Mercedes.'

He shrugged. 'What about your father's Land Rover?'

She stared at him in astonishment. When showing him over the practice she had not gone into detail about the vehicle stored in a garage at the back of the house, merely explaining that it hadn't been used for years and at some point she was going to have to dispense with it.

'The Land Rover's out of the question, I'm afraid.' She shrugged at his puzzled frown. 'It's not taxed or insured and I'm sure it won't even start.'

'I'll have a look at it,' he offered immediately. 'Insurance poses no problems. My company in London will oblige. Tax can be arranged as soon as we have the cover note — '

'No!' She stood up, her heart beginning to pound. 'No, thank you. I mean . . . I have every intention of part-exchanging it for another car.'

He looked surprised. 'But there's hardly any mileage on the clock, the bodywork is without blemish . . . If the mechanics are as good, it's almost a new vehicle. A swift overhaul would make it perfect for you.'

Elissa could no longer restrain herself. Not only did he persistently want his own way, but now he even proposed invading a part of her life which was utterly private!

'I have no intention of using the Land Rover, Adam. Only my father ever drove it. Please don't press me on the subject.'

He stiffened slightly. 'As you wish. But if you don't mind me saying, I think you're being unreasonable.'

'I don't need your advice!' she flared back, her cheeks burning. 'You're passing judgement on a subject you know absolutely nothing about.'

With the electricity snapping in the air almost enough to crackle, Elissa stalked off to the house.

Grace was in the kitchen. 'Problems?' she asked, frowning at Elissa's flushed face.

'One particular one!' Elissa retorted. She sank down into a chair as a strong cup of tea was put before her.

'Drink up,' Grace murmured, sitting down too.

Elissa paused before she said tightly, 'Sometimes I feel I'm fighting a losing battle with Adam.'

Grace shrugged. 'It's early days yet.'

'Adam suggested using Dad's Land Rover. Wouldn't let the subject drop.'

'Maybe it wasn't such a bad suggestion . . .'

Elissa turned to her in surprise. 'You sound as though you think I should consider it?'

'Perhaps consider the reasons why you won't.'

She shook her head, not understanding. 'Of course I don't want to use it, you must know that, Grace. The wretched thing brings back such miserable memories! Dad bought it brandnew to cheer Mum up while she was ill, thinking they would be using it together one day to make their calls. When she died, he was unable to bear the sight of it. His one extravagance and it turned out to be a terrible mistake!'

Grace nodded. 'For him, I think it symbolised all he loved and lost. But he's no longer here to grieve. There is nothing more in the world your parents would wish for you than happiness. Your father would be in despair if you continued to perceive your loss just as he had.'

Elissa bit down on her bottom lip. 'Perhaps you're right, but I really don't know . . .'

The older woman touched her arm. 'Think it over, Elissa.'

Elissa sighed, giving her a faint smile, wishing she could do just the opposite and for once stop thinking altogether.

That evening, unable to face the cold supper Grace had left for her, she went into the garden and unlocked the garage which housed her father's Land Rover. Adam must have come in and looked at it too for him to know the bodywork was good and the mileage low. But then, all the keys were kept on a board in the office, so it wouldn't have been difficult.

Elissa ran her hand over the sturdy green bonnet, cast her eyes to the unused seats, the untouched driving-wheel. From outside the garage, floating on the evening air, were sounds of life, real life: the evening blackbird, a plane droning overhead, someone mowing a lawn. Life.

Well, she had better start living it, hadn't she? a small voice said inside her.

Elissa discovered Adam in the house, replacing the receiver of the telephone. 'I've had a personal call from London,' he explained coolly. 'And I'm going into Farwell to make reservations for a friend to stay at the Saracen at the weekend.' There was a short pause before he added quickly, 'I won't be long.'

Elissa nodded. She hesitated. 'Adam, before you go . . . '

He stared down at her, his face tense.

'I feel I should explain about the Land Rover. Dad shut it away because he felt it had brought him bad luck. It was as though he shut away that part of his life. Mum died before they were able to use it, you see.'

His expression softened. 'I'm sorry. I wasn't trying to poke my nose into your business. I just wanted to help.'

Her skin grew warm under his gaze. 'I've thought it over. I think we should resurrect it.'

He looked at her doubtfully. 'Why the change of mind?'

'You were right, it's the perfect vehicle and it has been well-preserved even if it hasn't been used. I'm sure the garage will be able to fix it.'

He shrugged. 'OK. In that case I'll ring Farwell garage and have them take it into their workshops.' He paused. 'As a matter of fact, I wondered . . . Well, I thought perhaps what had happened earlier between us might still have been upsetting you.'

Trying to look as if what he was talking about was the furthest thing from her mind, she shook her head firmly. 'No, not at all.'

With a cool shrug he moved to the door, said goodbye briskly, and the next thing she heard was the Mercedes starting up.

Elissa stood in a bewildered silence, trying to analyse her feelings, her pounding heart at variance with the sensible reasoning she was trying to do.

Suddenly the phone rang. Elissa

picked it up distractedly.

'This is Minty Gale speaking,' announced a girl's husky voice. 'Is Adam there?'

'I'm afraid you've just missed him,' Elissa answered, wondering if she could catch him, but deciding she was too late. 'May I take a message?'

'Adam was going to arrange for me to stay in Farwell for a while in connection with my work. The point is, I wonder if you could ask him to book two rooms instead of one? I'm bringing a business partner with me.' A pause, then, 'That is Elissa, is it?'

'Yes ... it is.' Elissa said, curious now.

'The last time I spoke to Adam,' the caller remarked lightly, 'he couldn't stop singing your praises. I don't suppose he's mentioned me?'

'As a matter of fact, we haven't had time to discuss — ' Elissa began politely, but the girl broke in again.

'Adam and I were engaged, you see,' she explained coolly. 'It was before he went to America. Unfortunately the separation wasn't good for us — we called the engagement off. But now he's back in Britain to stay . . . Well, I'm confident we'll be able to get back together again.'

Elissa fell silent, turning the information over in her mind, suddenly wondering if Adam had used her to make his ex-fiancée jealous. After all, what other motive did he have for discussing her?

When Adam returned, Elissa explained Minty's request for changing the booking to two rooms.

Adam frowned as he stood in the hall. 'Philip Saville's probably coming with her. He's a commercial designer in the City and works with Minty on her contracts.'

'Minty is a designer?' Elissa asked.

He nodded. 'Quite talented, actually.' He hesitated. 'I knew her before I went to Los Angeles. She had begun to make quite a name for herself in interior design, though she can turn her hand to just about anything in the commercial world. She has that kind of artistic flair.'

He thrust a large hand through his hair. 'I'm afraid I had no luck at the Saracen. Booking rooms at this time of the year, for an indefinite period, is out of the question. Quite an inconvenience really, since Minty wants to be on the spot for her new contract — a manor house near Farwell she and Philip plan to transform before the place is opened to the public.'

Was it something or someone of a more personal nature that Minty wanted to be close to? Elissa reflected as she considered Adam's distracted expression.

Almost answering her question, he murmured, 'I suppose I could put them up in my flat for a short time. There's enough room. Would you have any objections, Elissa?'

If she had, Elissa found she was unable to voice them. Minty's and Adam's relationship was none of her concern, she reminded herself sternly as, giving her approval, she walked away, leaving Adam to make his arrangements.

4

Sharon arrived at eight-thirty the following morning, dressed in her green VN's uniform, her blonde hair pulled neatly back in a ponytail. Elissa was pleased to discover that the decorators had completed Reception and were working their way into the consulting-rooms and Adam's referral theatre.

'Perhaps if we begin with Trinka's and Honeybunch's diets,' Elissa suggested. 'I still give Honeybunch his milk mixture with his dextrose and amino acids. Minced beef, eggs and tripe and chicken are all refrigerated and have to be prepared first thing, along with Trinka's fruit and nuts and dried food.'

There was little doubt in Elissa's mind, as she discussed the day's routine with her new nurse, that Sharon was a perfect choice.

'If you'd like to have lunch with me

at one,' Elissa suggested, 'it will save you having to go back into Farwell.'

'And perhaps we can discuss some of your existing clients,' Sharon agreed eagerly, 'so I can familiarise myself with their cases?'

'Fine!' Elissa smiled, leaving Trinka and Honeybunch in Sharon's care. In Reception she discovered one early client.

'My name is Mrs Preston,' the woman announced, hauling herself up from her chair with difficulty, for she was as overweight as the dog at her side. 'This is my Labrador, Lavender. She's a bit plump, I know, but I'm sure she isn't pregnant and yet she has milk in her teats. It's making all her bedclothes damp. Each morning when I look in her basket there are big wet patches everywhere.' She tugged the lead to encourage the dog forward.

Elissa gestured to her consulting-room. 'Come along and we'll take a look.'

Lavender was far too heavy to hoist

on to the examination bench, but she was willing to sink to the floor and roll over.

Elissa listened to the Labrador's heart and found a healthy beat. Feeling all around the bitch's abdomen, she discovered no spherical swellings which would indicate pups.

'When did she last have her season?' Elissa asked with a frown.

Mrs Preston consulted her diary. 'Late in April. I made sure I kept her in and she went with no other dogs. Then she started to swell up and last month the little drops of milk began showing. It happened slightly last year as well, so I took no notice. Now, it's just getting worse.'

'She is in a pregnant state,' Elissa confirmed, examining the swollen mammary glands. 'But she hasn't any pups there, of course. You say she had a similar problem last year?'

Mrs Preston sank on to a chair, her florid face worried. 'Yes, but I knew she couldn't possibly be pregnant. And it only lasted a few weeks and seemed to dry up eventually. That's what I thought would happen this year.'

'Sometimes a condition occurs,' Elissa explained, 'called pseudopregnancy. Some unmated bitches ovulate, producing progesterone, as a pregnant bitch would. A small number of these bitches, of which Lavender seems to be one, have recurrent bouts after the same heat. Spaying is probably the best alternative to resolve the problem permanently.'

Mrs Preston shook her head vigorously. 'I don't want her to go through what I went through with my hysterectomy!'

Elissa smiled, understanding. 'For a woman it's quite different, I assure you. Lavender is the type of dog who would benefit from spaying if you don't want pups or continual phantom pregnancies. There are also other problems we must consider, such as pyometra — the presence of pus in the uterus — which can be brought about by this condition.'

'But she's only five!'

'And as she grows older, the danger

of a pyometra is ever-present,' Elissa gently warned.

'I'll think about it,' Mrs Preston mumbled, but Elissa felt she remained unconvinced.

'Mrs Preston . . . even if you were to decide to have her spayed, I'm afraid it would be impossible at the moment. She's far too overweight.'

The older woman's face flushed. 'I've tried to get it off, I really have. But both Lavender and I have the same problem.'

Elissa reflected that she had seen far too many overweight dogs in the last few weeks. People seemed to be killing their dogs with kindness.

'Firstly,' Elissa decided, 'I'm going to give Lavender an immediate injection of antibiotic to deal with the milk infection, and this is to be followed orally with ampicillin. Three capsules, twice a day for seven days. I'd like to see her again when the course is finished. This week I would like you to write down all that Lavender has to eat.

Make a list and bring it with you next week, when we'll go over it together and work out what is wrong.'

Mrs Preston looked crestfallen. 'Snacks don't help, I suppose?'

'Lavender shouldn't be having any food in between meals,' Elissa reproved gently.

'And nor should I, I suppose,' sighed the woman, looking down at her thick-ened waistline.

'Regular mealtimes are best for everyone,' Elissa said with a wry smile. 'Let's get the milk cleared up and then we can concentrate on diet. Don't allow her to lick herself or worry the teats. Put an old T-shirt over her and tie it so she can't get to lick them.' Elissa gave Lavender a pat and watched the overweight pair depart, wondering how she would ever persuade her client into a sensible eating routine for her pet, when she obviously found one impossible for herself.

Adam voiced her thoughts as he met her in the corridor. He looked back, frowning. 'One or two problems to be sorted out there, don't you think?'

Elissa nodded. 'I just hope next week I'm able to persuade her to put the dog on a sensible diet. Most of our clients with obese animals don't seem to be able to maintain their dogs on a healthy eating regime.'

'Then why don't you organise a weight-watching clinic?' he asked as he walked with her to the office. 'Weighing. Dietary advice on the importance of vigilance over an obese animal. Breaking down taboos on food. Helping people to understand calorie intake — fats, carbohydrates, proteins and so forth.'

'And perhaps a question-and-answer session,' Elissa agreed, suddenly enthused. 'After all, most pet owners, if they are female, will relate to slimming advice. The principle is the same, human or animal. Everything passed through here — ' she patted her stomach ' — materialises here!'

'I'm sure you don't ever have occasion to worry about weight,' Adam grinned, running his gaze over her. 'You're as slim as a reed.'

Elissa flushed. 'I'm lucky — I haven't a sweet tooth, which helps considerably.' Hurrying on to avoid his studied gaze, she added quickly, 'A weight-watching clinic would certainly be one way of solving a great many problems. Perhaps I'll give it a try.'

'You could hold a regular class here at the surgery,' Adam suggested immediately. 'We were going to advertise for another nurse. Perhaps this time we could find someone who is particularly interested in healthcare aspects to help you.'

Elissa paused. 'We had something fairly similar in a practice where I did part of my training fieldwork near Bristol. Not weight instruction particularly, but overall healthcare sessions.'

'And?' Adam's dark eyebrows creased questioningly.

'The idea was successful . . . on the whole.'

'But?' He frowned.

'Well, it worked very well because of each vet being able to delegate. It just seemed less personal, more functional, not like the days when — '

'Your father practised,' he put in, raising an eyebrow in wry enquiry.

She nodded. 'It sounds silly, I know . . . The medical scene has changed so much over the last few years. Doctors have less than five minutes for each patient in order to keep up with their appointments. The hospitals work flat out in order to cope with their lists — vets are on call night and day, even in a one-man practice, so I'm not unrealistic enough to think we can solve every client's problem instantly or even on a one-to-one basis, as it was in the old days. Group counselling has come into its own, I fully appreciate. But sometimes, I just wonder if the world is going just a little bit too fast for its own good.'

She fully expected him to come back with a sensible, highly logical response which her remark deserved, but instead he nodded thoughtfully. 'I'm inclined to agree with you. But if we can just keep a balance at Larkhill, the old ways mixed with the new — something for everyone — I think we'll build on our character and gain a reputation as a caring practice.' Then, dispelling all her illusions, he added firmly, 'Not forgetting, of course, that we have to run the practice as a viable concern!'

'Of course,' she answered crisply, and turned her gaze to Arnie, to hide her hurt feelings at the innuendo.

It was true; her father had lost all sight of reality and it was possible that Adam thought that she might have that tendency too, so she could hardly blame him for ramming home the point. She knew that it was essential to adapt, to move with the times. She also knew that a weight-watching clinic would solve a number of problems all ways round. But his manner still left her with a feeling of inexplicable resentment. However much she tried to think objectively, her head told her one thing and her heart another.

During the morning a Border collie named Breeze was presented to Sharon as having 'eye trouble'. Since Adam was busy with a client of his own, the case was referred to Elissa.

In accordance with the first rule of animal ophthalmoscopy, Elissa examined her patient's right eye with her own right eye, allowing the ophthalmoscope to act as a guard between her nose and the patient's.

Sharon set up an examination lamp and prepared the trolley with a binocular loupe, the ophthalmoscope and a rack of local anaesthetic and drops.

'If Adam's free now, I'd like him to come and have a look, Sharon,' Elissa said, pausing. She felt that the dog was clinically a poor case and warranted Adam's expert opinion.

In a few moments Adam appeared and began to examine the dog. 'Has the runniness become worse over the last week?' he asked, assessing any corneal damage to the unhealthy eye through his ophthalmoscope.

The owner, Mr McKenna, a small, jockey-built man with a cloth cap who kept sheep on his smallholding, explained that the eye had gradually become worse over several months. Breeze was unable to work in the fields now. He was afraid he had left bringing her in too late.

The few drops of local anaesthetic in the eye began to work. Breeze relaxed, and Sharon passed Adam the stain-like fluorescein which would reveal more of the cornea.

Adam nodded. 'A little more eyewash, please, Sharon, on the lids and surrounding hair, so we can keep the hair out of the way, temporarily at least.'

The careful examination took a further five minutes. 'It's a cataract problem,' Adam decided, straightening his back and turning to the man. 'I'll need her in for surgery, Mr McKenna.'

'Do you think you can save her sight?'

Adam paused thoughtfully. 'With

microscope surgery the chances of restoring some degree of sight are considerable. But I'm afraid I won't be able to tell you conclusively until after the operation.'

The owner picked Breeze up in his arms. 'I'm just lucky there's a specialist in the practice. Thanks a lot, Mr Kennedy.'

'She'll be staying at least one night with us,' Adam warned, 'maybe three or four, so Sharon will book you in for Wednesday at the latest. No breakfast for Breeze in the morning, or water, and she mustn't eat anything after eight o'clock the night before.'

When alone, Elissa recalled her client's observation. Mr McKenna had reminded her that having a specialist in the practice was undoubtedly an enormous advantage. Then, as though with a will of their own, her thoughts turned to Minty Gale. Adam hadn't mentioned the subject again and Elissa wondered when his guests were coming to Larkhill. Again a distracting ache nudged at her ribs when she thought of that soft, sexy voice on the line. She sounded a strikingly attractive female, if her voice was anything to go by. Elissa pictured her as rather exotic and dark-eyed, and wondered if her mental picture would tally with the real one.

Elissa ate lunch with Sharon; she had prepared sandwiches and they sat in deck-chairs in the garden. They talked of the morning's events and Elissa brought her new nurse up to date on as many clients as she could.

Then they sat quietly, taking in the sun and the cloudless sky. As Elissa closed her eyes under sunglasses, trying to keep her mind distracted from a recurrent picture of Minty Gale, she thought of the lovely landscape around her, of the day trippers who by now would be shading themselves under sunhats as they toured Stokesay Castle or paddled in the Severn as it coiled its way through the rich agricultural county where she had been born and bred. Why on earth Minty Gale should want a contract in this part of the world, so far from the sophistication of London, she couldn't begin to imagine.

Or could she?

*   *   *

Elissa changed into her theatre greens and proceeded to anaesthetise the tabby cat for spaying; clipping and shaving her flank, moving the sterile cloths to the surrounding areas. As she worked, she was conscious of the recently arrived removal van outside, the men shouting instructions to one another as the lorry disgorged furniture and crates. Their clatter through the surgery with Adam's equipment was distraction enough, and further compounded by yet another vehicle from Bensons which arrived in the drive.

'Heavens, what next!' Sharon laughed lightly as she handed Elissa the scalpel.

'Lucky we aren't doing major surgery,' Elissa sighed, trying to concentrate and finally making the incision. She began the search for the uterus and found it without delay, fixing artery forceps, clamping two arteries under the base of the uterus, to cut and snip and tie off.

She smiled at her nurse, the intensity of concentration a panacea to distraction. 'Don't mind me,' Elissa smiled. 'My nerves are just a little frayed with all the activity going on.

Sharon laughed. 'I find the refurbishment exciting, but I know it must be a nuisance for you at times.'

'It can't go on forever,' Elissa smiled ruefully. 'Now . . . One suture here and a couple along the skin flap, making sure the wound is left as neat as possible . . . And, yes, we're complete.' She turned and pulled down her mask. 'So you are really enjoying life at Larkhill, Sharon?'

'Oh, yes. And Adam's marvellous to work for isn't he?'

Elissa smiled ruefully. 'I'm glad you think so.'

They were interrupted by the insistent intercom ring in her consulting-room.

Elissa left Sharon to deal with the recovering cat and hurried in to answer it.

'It seems we have a mass invasion,' Adam said, amused. 'Are you coping?'

'I've just completed a spaying. Nothing else is urgent for the moment, is it?'

'Not surgically. Farwell garage have taken the Land Rover. Should have it back for Saturday. I've contacted my insurance company and you'll be fully covered as from today. And — er — don't concern yourself with the delivery vans; I've everything in hand.'

Of that she had no doubt! Elissa suppressed the urge to say so.

'Oh, yes,' he added swiftly. 'Mr Martin rang to say the hospital in Birmingham have called him in for Sunday. His op is next week. He asked about Arnie, of course. I simply said we had an ultra-sound to do, and at the moment he was responding well to the digoxin.'

'You seem to have everything under control,' Elissa couldn't resist snapping into the intercom.

Adam seemed not to notice. 'Just thought I'd check in. Over and out,' he said with a chuckle.

Elissa went back to Sharon and tried to compose her facial expression, hoping the irritation she was suppressing inside her was not as obvious as it felt.

* * *

The urgent call to Vale Farm came as a relief at the end of the afternoon. Elissa knew Gwen Richards, a client of her father's. Adam suggested she take the Mercedes and Elissa accepted, hoping a drive into the country would alleviate her tense mood.

Again she drove the car with special care. Elegant as the Mercedes was, she now found herself looking forward to the arrival of the Land Rover which, as Adam had remarked, was an ideal vehicle for the practice.

Recollecting this as the Mercedes hit

a deep crack in the lane, all thoughts were driven out of her mind as she saw Vale Farm's gate off its hinges, lying drunkenly on its side. Further on, the tractor had been driven into the barn askew and one of its huge tyres was deflated. The For Sale notice Elissa had seen in the lane was the biggest surprise. Vale Farm was to be auctioned off.

Sadly, as she drove in, Elissa remembered the place as a thriving concern, and, as a beef-producing farm, it had seen some of the finest cattle graze in its fields. Her father had known the couple who owned it and been their vet when times were good. In recent years though their need for a vet had dwindled until, last time she was home, her father had remarked that he had not visited the farm for over eighteen months.

Elissa knocked. It was some while before Gwen Richards managed to open the door. The frail, elderly woman walked aided by sticks, her arthritic legs barely getting her along.

In the kitchen, Elissa sat down to a cup of tea. She drank, listening with a sinking heart to Gwen's concern for her cow, Maddy, the only animal left on the derelict farm, reared as a calf by Gwen's youngest son.

'Should have asked you to come before,' Gwen sighed, with a racking cough. 'But I heard about your father. Didn't fancy changing to another vet. My neighbour called in this morning, said he'd phone you for me when he saw the state of Maddy.'

Gwen Richards's husband and eldest son had been killed in a car crash on their way to market. Their deaths had so shattered the surviving family that the remaining son, who had reared Maddy, had gone abroad in search of a new life. Gwen had been forced to continue the business on her own, but the task was beyond her as she suffered increasing ill health. She looked very frail now and the cough seemed to be particularly troublesome.

Elissa prepared to examine the cow. 'Have you no other stock left, Gwen?'

The older woman laughed, but no warmth came into her eyes. 'Up until last year I had hired help, but then I decided even a few head were beyond me. There was no use trying to hang on. But Maddy, well, as you know . . . she's special.'

Elissa picked up her case and looked around the dismal kitchen. Yellowing photographs of the family still adorned the mantlepiece. She recalled that the last time she had visited Gwen was with her father when she was on leave from Bristol, and then the place had still preserved something of a homely air about it.

Elissa examined Maddy, but knew even as she looked at her that the most humane course of action was to put her out of her discomfort.

'She has cystitis, Gwen,' Elissa explained gently as they stood with the animal in her shed. 'The infection has spread from her bladder up the ureters to her kidneys, hence her frequency in urination.'

Gwen Richards nodded. 'No matter what I've fed her, she's been losing weight too.'

Elissa sighed. There was nothing she could do, save for antibiotics, which, she was sure, had come too late now. 'The urine is extremely discoloured,' Elissa pointed out. 'I think antibiotics will have little or no effect.'

'Just try a short course,' Gwen pleaded, and, although it went against Elissa's better judgement, she agreed to do so.

She left Gwen leaning on her sticks, standing beside her cow. She drove back to Larkhill with a heavy heart, knowing with no doubt that soon she would return to attend to Maddy and relieve the poor animal of her struggle, but then there remained the greater and sadder human tragedy of a country-woman who had seen the demise of both her family and her livelihood.

She wondered just what her father

would have done had he been alive. He would, she was sure, have known exactly the right things to say and do and now she had a swift, sharp surge of deep loss.

Sitting in the car awhile to collect herself on her return to Larkhill, she made a mental note to call on Gwen soon and make an offer to help in any way she could.

★ ★ ★

The summer evening smelt wonderful as Elissa pushed open the French windows of her drawing-room. The lawn was dusted with evening sunlight and the scent of wild roses hung in the air. Elissa showered, washed her hair until it blazed with glints of red-gold and put on white trousers and a green silk shirt. She was tempted to make a long drink, and she crushed some oranges and ice, planning to sit out on the lawn and watch Honeybunch tumble in his pen.

Then the phone rang in the hall and, as there seemed no movement in the house, she hurried from her flat and picked up the receiver.

'Minty here,' said a female voice sharply.

Elissa took a slow breath. 'I'll find Adam for you.'

'Don't bother,' Minty said. 'It's not Adam I wanted. I'm just phoning to thank you for having us to stay.'

'That's quite all right,' Elissa answered politely, wondering when Larkhill was to be graced by Minty's presence.

'We'll be coming for the weekend,' Minty enlightened her. 'Adam says Larkhill is the most heavenly place.'

'Does he?' Elissa listened uneasily.

'Adam seems to be terribly happy there,' the voice went on effusively. 'I can't tell you how pleased I am he's settled. I feel quite confident now we can pick up where we left off with our relationship. Larkhill sounds the perfect setting.'

Elissa continued to listen in silence.

Eventually, when she put the phone down, there was no doubt in her mind that she had just been subject to a very clear message from Minty Gale.

'Was that Minty?' a voice asked behind her. She swivelled round to find Adam standing at the foot of the staircase. He wore a cream silk shirt and cream linen trousers and, with the light colour against his dark skin, he looked breathtakingly handsome. It was not hard to see just why Minty was attracted to him and why she had given an explicit warning to Elissa to keep well away. 'She phoned to thank you?' he asked before she could reply.

Elissa nodded. 'Your friend explained they will be arriving this weekend.'

He frowned. 'I'm sorry, I should have mentioned it. We were so busy I completely forgot. You're certain you don't mind them coming?'

'Why should I mind?' Elissa asked coolly. 'They're your guests, Adam. Larkhill is as much your home as it is mine. I'll have Grace put some fresh linen on the beds for you.'

'Thank you,' he murmured, walking with her to the door of her flat. Elissa was aware that the atmosphere seemed to shimmer with tension around them.

'Well . . . see you in the morning,' he said hesitantly. 'And — er — sleep well.'

For a moment she was sure that that was not what he had intended to say, and she paused before she stepped inside, her eyes meeting his for a few brief seconds. But he took a backward step and then strode to the staircase.

She closed the door, leaning her back against it with a deep sigh.

Minty Gale was now determined to win him back. Was he the kind of man who would forget their differences and begin their affair again?

One thing Elissa was certain of. She would not be used as a pawn between them, and the sooner she made that plain to Adam the better.

5

Adam was seated at his ophthalmic microscope, a piece of equipment which reminded Elissa of a ship's periscope, in the middle of the newly transformed theatre. Though the operating table beneath it was empty, Adam was concentrating so deeply on inspecting the equipment that he did not hear Elissa come in.

'Good morning,' she called, easing her way through the unopened wooden crates which were stacked in her path.

'Come in!' Adam looked up and slipped off the stool to push an obstacle from her path.

'You're busy.'

'Not at all. I was just checking everything had arrived from the storage people in London. All safe and sound, I'm pleased to say.'

'Will you have enough room in here?'

she asked, frowning at the crates.

'Oh, yes. Once I've unpacked and the decorators have removed their tables and ladders, yes, there'll be room to spare. All that remains is for the electricians to fit the Diotherm lamps and the clean air system.'

'Do you think you'll be ready for the middle of next week?' Elissa asked, already knowing the answer to her question, for she had learned by now that Adam rarely left anything to chance.

'Oh, yes,' Adam answered, predictably confident. 'I'll spend the next few days in here, setting up — and the decorators have agreed to work over the weekend too in order to complete the other theatre for next week's ops. Our diagnostic equipment is due to arrive later today . . . Yes . . . on the whole, I think we're doing rather well.'

Elissa frowned. 'You're going to spend the weekend setting up your equipment? But what about your guests?'

He hesitated before he answered her, rubbing his chin thoughtfully. 'I did explain the situation to Minty. She seems to think the contract they are working on at the manor house will take up most of their time. I'm sure they won't need much entertaining.'

Elissa had her doubts but, not expressing them, she left Adam and went in search of Sharon who had just finished feeding Trinka and Honeybunch.

Trinka waited patiently for her early-morning cuddle and, as Elissa drew her into her arms, the little chimpanzee grinned, revealing the rapid healing of the gums around her planed-down teeth. She allowed Elissa to sit her on an examination bench as Sharon held her and opened her mouth for a further inspection.

'She's healed perfectly,' Elissa said happily. 'She hasn't worried the dissolving sutures or picked at the teeth. I suppose it's almost time to return her to the wildlife park.'

Sharon opened her arms and Trinka leapt into them with a happy shriek before being returned to her cage. 'You're going to miss both of them, aren't you?'

Honeybunch pawed at his mesh cage and fell into his water-bowl. Elissa and Sharon burst into laughter. They bent over to stroke him. He grabbed their fingers, but this time he trapped Elissa's small hand with his teeth. Although he held it without viciousness, when she extracted it she saw that he had left a row of red indentations which, luckily, had not broken the skin.

'He needs playmates,' Sharon observed, frowning at the near-damage. 'He's outgrown his pen and he's bored. Even Jemima refused to go down and play with him this morning.'

Elissa nodded, rubbing her hand. 'Yes, both Trinka and Honeybunch will have to be returned soon, undoubtedly.'

Though she knew it was inevitable, Elissa felt saddened by her decision. The animals had been part of her life and her father's. They were the last animals he had treated and cared for and, when they went, a little part of her life went too.

Turning her thoughts to work, Elissa reflected that she had also come to a decision on the weight-watching classes. She could bring to mind at least half a dozen clients who had overweight pets and might very well be interested in the project. Once the class had begun, no doubt by word of mouth the idea would catch on.

As she went into the office, Adam forestalled her. 'Ah, before I begin this morning,' he said, handing her a file, 'I thought I would show you these.'

From the file she drew a buff-coloured envelope and sheet of headed notepaper, elegantly printed in scripted green with a neat emblem of Larkhill set to the right-hand side. The envelope was made out to 'Bruce', then an address, and once again the Larkhill logo was printed on the back of the envelope.

'It looks like an invitation,' Elissa commented.

'It is — our personal invitation, sent

to all our existing clients and to the new ones we have seen too. On each invitation will be logged Bruce's or Bonny's various details: vaccinations, boosters, recall dates. Plus information on post-dental cleaning, healthcare, flea control and worming. What do you think?'

'Are you asking for my opinion?'

'Yes, naturally.' Adam frowned at her.

'But you've had these printed already. It hardly seems to matter what I think!'

He shook his head. 'These are just a few examples. I simply thought we need to begin our PR as soon as possible, and what better than to have a few invitations printed up so we could look at them together?'

Elissa hesitated. She tried to dismiss the irritation she felt when Adam seemed to take matters into his own hands.

'I expected more enthusiasm,' Adam sighed as he saw her expression. 'Look. Let me explain. After each consultation we complete an advice note, a copy of which is kept with clinical records. This makes it very plain to us whether or not an examination is due or is necessary. Well, all I'm suggesting is that we send these out to our patients so they act as reminders and as a kind of insurance against illness.' He drew a long breath. 'Take Mr Martin, for instance. He brought Arnie to your father years ago for his first vaccinations. Then he allowed things to slide. If he had received one of these to jog his memory, he would no doubt have come in earlier and we would have diagnosed Arnie's condition before he became so sick.'

Elissa turned the invitation over in her hand. 'It's not that I disagree, not in principle . . . ' She shrugged lightly. 'You'd better have them printed up.'

The telephone rang and Adam turned to answer it. For a few minutes he listened, then, as he was explaining to a client how she might persuade her dog to take her pills orally, Elissa saw that it was an opportunity to leave. She was almost out of the door when she heard the phone go down and Adam call, 'Have you thought any more about the weight-watching clinic? We could add that to the list of healthcare facilities.'

She halted, giving a little sigh, wondering if Adam ever gave up. She turned, somewhat stony-faced, to look at him. 'Yes. I'm going to contact certain clients and set aside a time for next week.'

'Good!' he exclaimed enthusiastically. 'Now . . . what about an advertisement in the local paper and — '

Elissa flushed angrily. 'Thank you, I had thought of that, Adam. There are some things I can handle reasonably efficiently by myself!'

He caught her arm as she almost made the hallway. 'Elissa, I didn't mean to imply — '

She pulled her arm free. 'Don't you think you have more than enough on your own agenda with your referral unit and your weekend guests without trying to tell me how I should be functioning?'

It was a childish, ill-chosen comment,

she realised as she left the office, hurrying along to her own room. She did not want him to think she was disturbed by the fact that he was hosting visitors. Larkhill was as much his home now as it was hers. But inside, she fought a battle, one she was powerless to understand fully and, although she did not know why, Adam just seemed to provoke her.

By the time six o'clock came, most of the new diagnostic equipment had been delivered and she had added two more names of patients whom she saw that afternoon to her list of those with weight-related problems.

She did not see Adam that evening as, remaining in her flat, she conquered her restlessness by concentrating on long-overdue housework. Hearing Adam's light footfall on the stairs late at night, she knew she had assumed correctly that he would have worked late in his unit.

The next morning two routine cases of puppy vaccinations and a minor wound on a scored pad brought her to the close of an uneventful surgery.

Elissa had bidden Adam good morning briefly as the decorators had arrived, wondering what time his guests were due. It was not long before she found out, as, just after midday, going into Larkhill by the connecting door, she discovered for herself.

In the hall, a young woman stood close to Adam, her hand resting on his shoulder, his arm at her waist. At the sudden intrusion, they broke apart and Minty Gale turned towards Elissa and smiled. 'Hello, Elissa.' She held out a slender hand. 'I've been so looking forward to meeting you!'

The girl was stunning, with hair as dark as Adam's flowing to her shoulders. She had very deep brown eyes and pale, china-like skin.

Elissa found herself making polite conversation as Adam stood silently, his hands pushed deeply in his pockets.

'Has your colleague come with you?' Elissa asked eventually, hoping that her embarrassment at having discovered Minty and Adam in each other's arms did not show on her face.

'Philip?' Minty shrugged. 'Oh, yes. He's gone into Farwell to buy you some flowers. I'm afraid we came awfully empty-handed.'

Elissa wondered if Philip had proposed the flowers or had been sent on an errand for reasons which were best known to Minty and Adam.

'I must go now,' Elissa said, as the conversation seemed suddenly to come to an end. 'No doubt we'll bump into each other later.'

'You can spare time to have lunch in the garden with us, surely?' Adam asked, as Minty turned to frown at him.

'I'm afraid not.' Elissa had no desire to play gooseberry and, if her suspicions had been correct initially regarding Adam's intentions of arousing Minty's jealousy, she would steer well clear of compromising situations. 'I have Trinka and Honeybunch to clean,' she murmured as a poor excuse.

'Can't they wait until after lunch?' Adam raised a dark, questioning eyebrow. 'I'll give you some help then.'

Elissa shook her head. 'I can manage quite well, but thanks anyway.'

'Perhaps we can all have lunch another time,' Minty suggested, and Elissa nodded, staring into the brown eyes which so clearly gave the message that Minty had no other intention but to have Adam to herself.

Elissa escaped to the surgery. After being targeted by Minty, she hadn't the least desire to stay where her company was not wanted.

At last, with the cleaning of Honeybunch and Trinka completed, Elissa longed for a shower, but hesitated to go back into the house. She sat with a sigh in the office chair, stroking Jemima who consented, for once, to be cuddled. Unable to concentrate, Elissa reviewed her options. She couldn't go back into her flat, for the French windows opened on to the garden and there Adam and Minty would be. Here in the surgery she could not keep from under the feet of the decorators, but neither could she escape to Farwell, for the Land Rover had not yet been returned.

Jemima suddenly hissed and scooted off the desk. The door opened and Arnie padded in, followed by a tall blond man, half obscured by a huge bouquet of summer flowers.

'Hi, there! It's Elissa, isn't it?'

She nodded as the gorgeous bouquet was pressed into her arms.

'Philip Saville,' grinned the handsome stranger. 'I've come to — er — find Cinderella?'

Elissa found herself laughing, the recipient of the disarming wit of Larkhill's second guest, who, perched casually with one thigh on the corner of her desk, introduced himself. 'I accompany Minty on certain contracts, look over the specifications of the contract for her, work out how long it will take to complete the necessary renovations, et cetera. She is the artistic talent, I'm just the boring business end.' He gestured to a tweed jacket he had thrown over a chair. 'I'm supposed to be wearing it, on Minty's orders,' he grinned, 'to look the part. But to be honest, I'm an admirer of the country, not a partaker.'

Elissa grinned. 'The country's not too bad when you get used to it . . . Mostly jeans here, or shorts and shirts, anything casual. I hope you've brought a change with you or you'll fry in a tweed jacket.'

'So I don't have to wear it to impress you?'

Elissa laughed. 'No need at all.'

He was an exceptionally good-looking man, in his late twenties or early thirties, Elissa conjectured as they talked. Too much of an outright Romeo to be attractive to her, and yet he made her smile.

'How come you're not eating lunch?' he asked, his blue eyes running over her admiringly.

Elissa shrugged. 'One of us is always on call over the weekend . . . '

'I'll believe you,' he chuckled as she floundered. 'Though if I were to risk a guess, I'd say you were keeping out of the way, deliberately.' He arched a blond eyebrow inquisitively. 'You know Adam and Minty were engaged once?'

She nodded. 'Yes.'

'She's still very much attracted to him.'

'I really wouldn't know,' Elissa said distantly, getting to her feet to shuffle the papers in front of her. 'Now I really must get on — '

'And Adam's a very attractive man,' Philip persisted.

Elissa tensed. 'Adam is my practice partner — we work together — that's all, Philip.'

'Oh, like Minty and me?' He laughed ruefully, fair eyebrows jerking up.

'Philip — ' she began, but stopped as he stretched out a hand and laid it on her arm.

'I'm only joking; don't take me too literally!'

142

'I won't,' Elissa promised him firmly, her face grave.

He laughed at her expression, allowing his hand to remain on her arm. 'Once you and I get to know each other a little better — '

Just then, Adam strode in. 'I see you found your way around,' he said curtly to Philip. 'Minty is waiting at the car. You've both a busy schedule this afternoon, I understand.'

Her companion shrugged lightly, in no hurry to drop his fingers from Elissa's arm. But when he did so, he laughed lightly. 'I was just trying to tempt Elissa to some lunch.'

'I've tried already,' Adam bit back tightly. 'But of course, you might have had more luck.'

'Not in the least.' Philip walked to the door. 'Well, see you later, Elissa. Don't work too hard.'

As both men left the room, Elissa harboured the distinct impression that neither man liked the other. Though Minty and Philip were business partners, they were obviously friends. But did Adam read more into their relationship, and was his dislike for the good-looking man based on rivalry? It was a suspicion which grew into certainty as she began to tidy her things away.

Before long, she heard the rumble of a diesel engine. Elissa went into Reception. From one of the big windows she saw her father's green Land Rover being parked beside a rather spectacular white Porsche. Philip climbed into the driver's seat of the Porsche as Adam stood to one side.

A long, slim arm waved from the Porsche's passenger window. A few seconds later the car was gone, and a garage mechanic clad in green overalls jumped from the Land Rover. She saw Adam walk around it, and the mechanic handed him the keys and, after a short discussion, left in another car which had followed the Land Rover in.

Elissa walked out into the bright sunshine. Adam handed her the set of keys. 'All done. Serviced and all necessary new parts fitted. What do you think?' He went down on his haunches, inspecting the tyres.

Elissa hesitated. 'I hope it was the right thing to do.'

Adam glanced up at her. 'I know how difficult the decision was, but you won't regret it, I promise you.'

She nodded, smothering the little tug at her heart as she looked at the Land Rover.

'I've been thinking,' Elissa said suddenly, 'about Honeybunch and Trinka. The Land Rover is an ideal vehicle to transport them back to the wildlife park.' She looked at Adam under her lashes. 'I've really no excuse to keep them now.'

He stood up, studying her carefully. 'I don't suppose that was a particularly easy decision for you either?'

'It had to be made. Yesterday I realised just how strong Honeybunch is becoming. With only Trinka and Jemima to entertain him and very little space, I would be doing the animal an injustice if I kept him any longer.'

Adam nodded, watching her. 'Have you contacted the park?'

'I'm going to. This afternoon.'

'Well, if they agree to have them back this weekend, I'll drive you over, if you like. I can fix up the back of the Land Rover for Honeybunch — construct a ramp from the pen to the tailboard. And perhaps you can sit with Trinka in the front. She's quite happy if she's in your arms — we can put a safety harness on her which you can hold on to, just to make sure she doesn't fly out of the window.'

Elissa looked up in surprise. 'But what about the preparation of your unit? Plus you have your . . . ' She stopped, flushing slightly.

He grinned. 'And I have my visitors to amuse, you were going to say? Well, as far as playing host goes, Minty and Philip don't expect VIP treatment. There are any number of restaurants for them to choose from, so they won't starve. And as for my unit, I'm well ahead of schedule. I managed to get much more done last night than I expected.' He took her arm, steering her back to the practice. 'Go and make your phone call. Strike while the iron's hot. If you need me, I'll be in my unit.'

He smiled again as he left her and, slightly breathlessly, Elissa decided she could not turn back now and picked up the phone in the office to call the wildlife park.

She had half hoped there would be a hitch. But, on hearing that the wildlife park had just acquired two other fully weaned cubs from zoos which were about to close, Elissa knew there was no longer any doubt.

She went in search of Adam. When she looked in his room the scene had changed vastly from yesterday. The microscope was fully in position; so too was the machine which operated it, standing nearby, its technology waiting to receive all the commands of the ophthalmologist when it was fully switched on. Adam was arranging more optical diagnostic equipment on the other side of the room and above him was the blank video screen on which, when an operation was in progress, his intricate movements would be fully shown.

'My goodness, a different room from yesterday,' Elissa gasped, stepping in. 'How have you managed it?'

Adam shrugged modestly. 'I've had enough experience with ophthalmic equipment in my time. In the States, they have nothing but the best in health care and it's very difficult not to become obsessed with each new piece of technology brought on the market.' He gestured to the microscope. 'But this really is the *pièce de résistance*. The microscope has transformed ophthalmology. I have to admit I wouldn't want to operate without one now. You see, when I'm looking into the microscope lens I feel as though the machine is an extension of my mind and fingers. I'm nowhere else in the theatre, just there, all my senses focused wholly on my patient's eye, knowing I can achieve a degree of clinical success that only a few years ago would have been considered impossible.'

Elissa nodded, realising that he became truly alive when he talked about what was closest to his heart. 'You make it seem so exciting. Did you always want to specialise in ophthalmology?'

He paused as he thought. 'My father encouraged me, I think, initially. He made me aware of just how vital sight is, possibly the last sense we would choose to lose if we were forced to make such a decision, which of course we aren't. But without sight, a human or an animal is completely incapacitated. For those who are deaf, there is still colour, night and day, movement, visual contact with the world, but once the optical blind has been drawn, the night is perpetual, unrelieved.'

Elissa drew a deep breath, touched by his words. Often she had wished she had been able to do more for an animal: one such as Breeze, whom she had referred to Adam. And now it was within her power to help, if not directly through her own hands, by Adam's skills. Her father would have been impressed — no, more than that! He would have wanted this for Larkhill, and suddenly she felt a warm glow inside her.

She gazed at him in silence for a few minutes, then dragged her mind back to the question in hand. 'I've phoned the wildlife park. They will take Trinka and Honeybunch. Tomorrow afternoon, actually.'

'Fine by me.' Adam watched her with his dark, speculative gaze.

'I don't really want to bother you, Adam — '

'It's no bother. You'll need some help with two animals.' He saw her indecision and frowned. 'Elissa, this is a partnership. For heaven's sake stop acting as though you were trying to carry the whole weight of the world on your shoulders. I want to help. I want to . . . share, not intrude — or manipulate.' He looked at her reproachfully. 'Can't you trust me?'

She just could not understand herself, for she wanted to trust him, needed to, but still in the back of her mind there were doubts and a deeper unease, so deep she could not fully bring it to the surface. She recalled the way he had kissed her, the feel of his lips on her mouth and the feel of his dark hair in her fingers. She had to fight an impulse to want that kiss all over again as her gaze ran to the deep brown well in his throat and the little pulse beating fast there. And then she thought of Minty, and reality slipped back into focus again.

'About late morning, then?' Elissa mumbled.

He nodded. 'Late morning it is.'

She hurried out of the room and along the hallway so rapidly that she almost fell over Arnie, who was waiting for Adam. Back in her flat she jammed her door shut, her heart refusing to subside to a slower pace.

Elissa found it difficult to sleep that night. OK, he had kissed her once, but surely she mustn't let it get out of perspective! A mutual attraction, a sudden, inexplicable impulse had gripped them both, hers being a purely physical response to an intensely attractive male. Presumably he had felt some degree of attraction for her too. But it was only momentary, and to build it up out of proportion as she was doing threatened their already tenuous partnership.

★ ★ ★

'I've constructed a ramp leading out from Honeybunch's pen and made a bed of straw in the rear compartment, with hay bales at either side so he won't fall about,' Adam explained next morning as he stood in the garden by the pen. 'We'll hoist the ramp up to the tailboard, then Honeybunch can simply walk along it, though I daresay he will need a little encouragement.'

Jemima leapt on to the wall nearby and pressed her blue tail into the air.

'She's picking up the vibes,' Elissa sighed, feeling jaded from the restless night. Trying to keep all her concentration on Honeybunch and not Adam's supple body, clad in dark blue shorts, leaning over the pen, she asked, 'It's Mr Martin's by-pass on Monday, isn't it?'

'Yes, we'll ring in later,' Adam called, unaware of her studied gaze, levering the tailboard to the back of Honeybunch's pen and slipping a ramp through the gate. 'Well, are you ready for the maiden voyage?' he turned to ask with a grin.

Elissa nodded, steeling herself inwardly for the journey. She went back into the surgery to find Honeybunch's feeding-bottle to tempt him. The cub still adored it and, though he did not drink from it, his attention was caught at its reappearance.

With Adam standing by, Elissa led Honeybunch with the bottle, nose to teat, up the ramp. The only obstacle proved to be Jemima, who jumped in too at the last moment and refused to be caught.

Finally retrieving her, Adam presented to Elissa a disgruntled cat, her blue fur spiky and her midnight eyes shrinking to tiny slits of angry displeasure.

'She never was a cuddly cat,' Elissa

grinned, as Jemima hissed spitefully and wriggled free, brandishing a paw. 'But she's been surrogate mum to so many orphaned animals, she doesn't like to see one of her brood go.'

Adam thrust a hand through his dark hair. 'A big wrench,' he agreed. 'Though Honeybunch isn't exactly the run-of-the-mill orphan!'

Next was Trinka, who, happy with so much attention focused on her, allowed a harness to be slipped over her head and snugly around her chest, the lead attached firmly to Elissa's wrist. There was no need for concern, for, once in an embrace, Trinka rarely moved, but locked her hands around Elissa's neck. Reflecting that it had been wise to wear cool linen trousers and a shirt of the same weight, Elissa wished she had tied her loose, freshly washed hair back in safety too. Trinka however made the most of the opportunity by burying her lips in it.

As they drove, Elissa's gaze descended to the tiny Saint Christopher glued on the facia by her father. She tried not to feel saddened by the memory, chewing down on her bottom lip to focus her attention on the road.

Suddenly, Adam's hand came across and squeezed hers, his dark eyebrows raised. 'OK?' he asked simply.

'I'm fine,' she mumbled and then, as Trinka pounded his hand with her knuckles, they both laughed.

Adam returned his gaze to the road. All the way to the wildlife park, Elissa's pulse seemed to be running fast as she tried hard to relax.

When Adam pulled into the enclosure, a keeper met them. He shook hands with Adam and explained that they had two new lion cubs, orphans like Honeybunch. 'These two are slightly older than Honeybunch,' he told them, after Adam had backed the Land Rover into the special compound and flipped down the tailboard for Honeybunch to descend. Elissa looked through the wire partitioning in the Land Rover. Honeybunch lazily swaggered down the ramp and into his new pen, where, through another mesh fence, he could see two more cubs looking at him with equal curiosity. 'Honeybunch will be integrated with them slowly, and in a day or two he'll have settled,' the keeper assured Elissa.

She nodded, feeling relieved for the three healthy cubs who had survived in a difficult world. In the wild, alone, they would have died. At least being born in captivity had given them a chance of survival.

'He's settling well,' Adam reassured her as they drove to the monkey enclosure.

She nodded as she hugged Trinka. 'I can't help thinking back on Honeybunch's short life. All that life-saving dextrose and amino acids introduced into his little jugular by drip in the first difficult days. Each infusion took Dad at least an hour, three times a day. Then he had to introduce cow's milk and additives by stomach tube.' She gave a small sigh, thinking of all the care her father had lavished on the animals he had been so committed to in his life.

'Lucky for the world there are men like your father,' Adam remarked, as they arrived at Trinka's home. Safely parking at the rear, Adam and Elissa went in the back way with Trinka, following the keeper named Rolf who was her father's old acquaintance at the park.

When Trinka saw her enclosure, she wriggled to free her long arms and legs from Elissa's restraining hold.

'She's pleased to be back,' the keeper laughed, catching hold of Trinka. 'I'll take her in.'

'She's lost none of her acting skills,' Adam observed, as the cheeky chimp leapt from Rolf's arms on to a tree branch, making faces at the group of children who gazed in through the wire mesh.

'You've done a grand job on her teeth,' Rolf said as he came out, locking the door securely behind him.

Trinka did not even turn to give Elissa a toothy smile. She was too busy checking the familiar objects of her normal life and calling to her two companions, who looked curiously on from the far side of the enclosure.

Rolf said gently, 'Your father and I had many long chats. He didn't like to see wild animals caged, but he knew it was a way of introducing children to a whole new world — and he knew the animals were all well looked after too.'

Elissa nodded as she beat down a pang of sadness. 'I think from the first time he brought me here I always wanted to see Africa for myself, discover where these beautiful creatures really came from.'

Adam touched her arm softly. 'Time to go, I think.'

For the final time, they glimpsed Trinka who, in her usual style, was flaunting her charms at the mesmerised children. Having said a last goodbye, in the warm sunshine outside Adam smiled down at her. 'Well, all over now. You could see how happy Trinka and Honeybunch were. And you can also be very proud of yourself and your father for the work you did with them.' The sun shone through his dark hair, and his deep brown eyes gazed softly down at her.

She nodded, looking up into his gaze. 'Yes, I know I couldn't keep them at Larkhill forever.' She laughed lightly. 'It's a good job I'm not the park's vet. They'd be missing half their animals!'

He laughed too, then, still smiling, he said, 'I was wondering . . . Would you like to have dinner out this evening? We could ask Harry to take calls for us.' To her dismay he added, 'I thought I'd book a table for four around eight?'

Hot colour flooded her cheeks as she realised Adam's intention. Elissa shook her head. 'I'm sorry, but no.'

'What is it?' he asked with a deep frown. 'What have I said?'

'I won't be used, Adam,' she told him truthfully. 'Please understand that.'

Deep lines showed in his forehead. 'Used? What on earth do you mean? Elissa, you've misunderstood me — '

'Have I?' She shook her head slowly. 'I don't think so.'

He stiffened, his dark eyes wary. Then he shrugged, his face white. 'If you want to take such an attitude, then so be it. But I can't begin to understand why you're making life so difficult, Elissa, when, after all, an evening out on the town would probably go a long way to improving our relationship.'

6

Elissa paused thoughtfully as she looked over some of her notes; her mind insisted on returning to last night. She wondered if Adam had enjoyed what he called his 'evening out on the town'. Having retreated to the safety of her apartment, and spent most of the evening washing her hair and soaking in a foamy bath while playing some soothing background music, she had persuaded herself that she couldn't be less interested in what Adam did or didn't do with Araminta Gale!

But Monday had brought with it renewed mental disquiet as, listening carefully, she heard Adam's deep voice in Reception. Sharon's reply echoed too amid the breezy salutations of the decorators.

Arnie padded in, sniffing Elissa's hand. She stroked him fondly, looking up to see Adam.

'Good morning.' His dark eyes surveyed her levelly without any hint of their last meeting.

'Good morning, Adam.'

'Have you seen the main theatre yet?' he asked as he tugged on his white coat, pulling it smartly into place over green cords and checked shirt.

'No. I was just on my way to look.' Elissa gestured to the door, aware of the cool politeness between them. They walked along the passageway to the theatre, opening the door to see the two new operating tables, one positioned next to the mobile anaesthetic machine, and in the furthest corner the brand new ultra-sound, all surrounded by shining white walls.

'I think Mr Rumble's team did pretty well in the short time allotted.' Adam amused himself with turning dials on the ultra-sound, smiling in quiet satisfaction.

Noticing his reaction, Elissa found herself breathing a sigh of relief too.

She had been imagining the worst kind of scenario: a long list of casualties with no operational operating theatre! 'I really wouldn't have believed it,' she murmured with a soft sigh.

'Oh ye of little faith!' Adam grinned as he glanced at her.

'And I suppose you didn't imagine a backlog of ops waiting at the door for instant treatment?' Elissa teased, relief making her light-hearted.

'I had full confidence in our man with the briefcase!' Adam chuckled, as he walked around the room, finally coming back to stand beside her. 'Well, shall we bring in Arnie and make him first on our list?'

The atmosphere had grown lighter, Elissa realised, and rightly so, for this week should be one of professional triumph since, working against the clock, the surgery was halfway complete and Adam's unit almost finished into the bargain.

Arnie was persuaded in and positioned by the ultra-sound. While Adam prepared the machine, Elissa eased the dog into recumbency, clipping an area of his coat so that the transducer could make good contact with his skin.

Squirting some aquasonic gel to help transmission of the ultra-sound waves, Adam began to scan.

On the video screen they watched the outline of the heart and its ventricles, the left one appearing dilated.

'The blood has been regurgitated back from the left ventricle into the left atrium, increasing its enlargement,' he remarked thoughtfully. 'I'll freeze the picture and measure the diameter of different chambers. Then we can compare them with known values of a healthy dog of Arnie's size.'

Elissa watched him quietly and contentedly, extremely grateful for the balm of work and the gradual easing of the tension which had threatened them first thing.

After giving Arnie a full scan, Adam considered the heart-chamber measurements. 'Enlarged, but not as much as I feared,' he sighed in relief. 'The digoxin we started him on last week has reduced the tachycardia, which is a very good sign.'

'So for now we shall keep him on digoxin and add no other drug?'

He nodded. 'Provided we see no deterioration in his condition, yes.'

Elissa paused. 'You know, I thought he might fret with anxiety over being left, but he seems to have settled . . . Perhaps because he's in the office with us during the day and in the evenings he's with you. He's with company virtually all the time.'

Adam frowned as though she had touched a sore point. 'Yes, true . . . Though last night I was obliged to put him out of the lounge, which he didn't appreciate very much. Minty is allergic to his hair, which does seem to come out in handfuls.'

Poor dog, Elissa thought. He couldn't help his hair-loss, probably made worse by his condition. As Arnie lethargically descended to the floor, Adam smoothed his grey head. 'I've suggested Minty ask her doctor for an antihistamine which might help to cure the allergy . . . '

Elissa realised there was not too much hope in his voice. She also recollected noticing Minty brushing the hair from her clothes, picking the stubborn ones off individually, unable to disguise her dislike of them. However, it was not for her to say and, as Adam made no more comment, the subject was dropped.

As he packed the ultra-sound away and Elissa cleaned the tranducer of its gel, suddenly Sharon appeared, peering hesitantly around the theatre doors. 'Adam, a young lady is waiting to see you. She says — '

Minty appeared, cutting the young nurse short. She was wearing a stunning white jogging suit noticeably free of dog-hair. 'I've been looking for you everywhere, Adam!' she exclaimed with a sweet smile.

Adam cast her a swift glance, then turned to Sharon. 'It's all right, Sharon, we have finished in here actually.'

When Sharon had gone, Minty slid her hand through Adam's arm. 'We were sorry you couldn't join us last night, Elissa. We had a wonderful time. Adam, you must see to it that Elissa comes when we next go out.' She looked under her dark lashes at him. 'While I'm here, will you take me around your new surgery and show me the referral unit?'

Adam glanced at his watch. 'Our appointments start shortly . . . '

'But it will only take a few moments. Philip and I have to be on our way soon too.'

Elissa decided it was time to make herself scarce. She slid past them into the corridor, almost bumping into Sharon.

'Your client,' Sharon explained. 'Shall I send her in?'

'Yes, of course.' Elissa hurried to her room and, taking a levelling breath, she greeted her client, a young woman with a chihuahua. The little dog had scratched his ear so badly that he had made it bleed.

Elissa cleaned the wound and trimmed his nails, the cause of the damage, avoiding the nippy white teeth which bared at her as soon as she applied antiseptic.

'There's no infection,' Elissa explained. 'Keep it clean and bathe it each day. I'll prescribe an antiseptic lotion which should clear it up.'

Just as client and patient were leaving, Adam arrived back from his tour, gently holding out his hand to the tiny dog. Minty shrank behind him, her eyes glued to the wound. 'I can't bear the sight of blood,' she gasped, her lovely face stark white against her black hair.

There was absolute silence as she sighed and sagged into Adam's arms.

Five minutes later, Minty was rousing as she sat in a chair in the office, Elissa holding a glass to her lips.

'How are you feeling?' Adam asked worriedly.

'Better, thank you.' Minty delicately wrapped her fingers around Adam's strong hand. 'I think the smell of all this disinfectant doesn't help.' She clung to

Adam as he helped her up, and Elissa watched them walk slowly into Reception. Minty looked as fragile as Dresden china in Adam's arms, quite different now from the stony-eyed adversary she had been earlier.

'She's a wonderful girl, isn't she?' came the soft, sardonic voice beside her.

Elissa found herself gazing into twinkling blue eyes. 'Philip, where did you spring from?'

'I got lost trying to keep up with Minty and Adam on the guided tour,' he laughed easily. 'Adam was showing us over the theatre conversion. I've only just managed to extricate myself from an enthralling and utterly unfathomable discussion on damp courses with a decorator!'

Elissa found she was laughing too, but drawing a deep breath, she sighed, 'Minty almost fainted.'

'Conveniently into Adam's open arms, I would guess,' Philip murmured with irony. Taking a long look at her, he remarked, 'We haven't seen much of you lately. Don't tell me you've been working all the time, because I shan't believe you. Last night you missed a superb meal!'

To confess she had deliberately gone into hiding would have been less than polite, but Elissa found it difficult to look her visitor in the eye and not admit the truth.

'Don't worry.' He smiled wryly at her hesitation. 'I won't press you, but next time I insist — '

'Philip!' a familiar voice called.

'Minty has obviously quite recovered!' He grinned at Elissa. 'Catch you later. And this time, I mean it.'

Elissa watched him hurry off to join Minty, giving a small sigh of relief. She had had the feeling he was about to suggest another foursome, and if just one more person did that she would scream!

Sharon sent in the next client, a woman leading a large brown dog with an incredibly shaggy coat. Under a full fringe, the dog blinked at Elissa with rather a dull expression.

'He's a Briard, isn't he?' Elissa asked, recognising the unusual French herding dog.

The woman nodded. 'Oscar's six now, but he doesn't seem to see stationary objects. Sometimes he bumps into things which are quite obvious, like a leg or a post.'

Elissa examined the eyes with her ophthalmoscope. She discovered a brown pigment just beginning to creep over the right retina. The other eye was not yet affected.

'Have you noticed any problems with sight before?'

The woman hesitated. 'Sometimes when we've thrown the ball he hasn't been able to find it, though his sense of smell usually takes him there. I've noticed the bumping into things for about a year, but I thought he was just being clumsy.'

Elissa recognised the complaint instantly as progressive retinal atrophy. However, she did not want to alarm the woman as there were several forms of the disease, some of which were less serious than others.

'I would like to have a second opinion on Oscar,' Elissa explained carefully. 'He may have a problem with his middle vision. Sometimes certain breeds are apt to have an inherited condition.'

'Oh, that's not possible with Oscar!' protested the woman. 'We paid an awful lot of money for him. Briards are not inexpensive dogs, you know.'

Elissa patted Oscar, who wagged his tail happily, reflecting that simply because a dog cost a great deal of money, it was no guarantee when it came to health, a fact many people were ignorant of when selecting a pet. Persuading the woman to make an appointment with Sharon for Adam's referral clinic later in the week, she wondered if he would draw the same conclusions and how the client would respond to a diagnosis of PRA, which, almost always, was a genetic legacy donated from one of the dog's parents.

Later in the day, Adam discovered her in the recovery-room. He nodded towards the empty pen of Honeybunch. 'Have you rung the wildlife park to see how they are?'

She shook her head. 'No, I'm sure we would have heard if there were any problems.'

'It seems quiet without them, doesn't it?' He was looking at her with concern, and she flushed. She had been trying to keep her mind off the empty pens all day.

'I'm growing used to it,' she smiled with a small sigh.

'You should have come out last night and taken your mind off work.' Adam grinned ruefully. But, as her green eyes sparkled on the subject of last night, he added swiftly, 'Actually, I didn't come to talk about last night, but something far more important. I think I've found a person who might fit the bill for our other nurse. A Mrs Barbara Thomas who's just moved to Farwell. She brought in her terrier, Blimp, this morning for boosters and during the course of the conversation I discovered she's a trained veterinary nurse. All her children are at school now and she's looking for something part-time.'

'Has she any experience in pet healthcare?' Elissa asked, very surprised at this bit of luck.

He nodded. 'Luckily enough, yes. Before moving she took a refresher course at college in animal nursing.' He edged towards the door, raising his thick eyebrows. 'Mrs Thomas is in Reception. Come and meet her!'

Elissa paused, trying to conquer the sense that she was being yet once again driven along in another direction altogether, for only this morning she had phoned the *Gazette* and put in an advertisement for Friday. Perhaps it was a good idea to meet Mrs Thomas, though. Nothing could be lost, she supposed, but all the same she felt reluctant as she walked with Adam to Reception.

Mrs Thomas, however, dispelled her qualms immediately by holding out her hand and greeting Elissa with a bright smile. She carried a small Jack Russell under one arm, his little black eyes glinting at Elissa as she patted his soft head.

'Why don't we talk in the garden?' suggested Adam. 'We've no clients at the moment and it's far too beautiful a day to miss.'

They left the surgery and went by the side of the house through the gate. 'What a lovely old tennis-court,' Barbara sighed. 'It's such a beautiful garden! You should see ours. A complete wreck with all the children's things.'

'Larkhill has seen very few children,' Elissa explained as they sat on the white patio chairs and little Blimp jumped down to sniff the lawn, zipping through Arnie's long legs. 'I had no brothers or sisters, but of course there were always animals. The kennels are just over there behind the laurel hedges. There's even a stable too where we kept a small pony. Dad hired the field from the farmer across the road, so I didn't have far to go to graze him.'

'Oh, I'm afraid we didn't have a pony, or even a dog,' Barbara sighed. 'I'm from a family of four — three huge brothers and me — and that was enough for Mum and Dad to cope with. I seem to be carrying on the tradition. Our youngest is six,' Barbara counted, pushing back her neat brown hair, 'the next is eight and the oldest twelve. But I'm going to stop there. I've been in nappy-land for too long. I'm really looking forward to getting back to work.'

Elissa explained the project she was going to concentrate on: nutrition and dietary management. She liked Barbara Thomas and, in spite of her initial reluctance to share Adam's enthusiasm, she found she had decided Barbara was the kind of person who would fit in very well at Larkhill.

'Weight Watchers?' Barbara mused. 'I've been to a few myself, but it would be interesting to run an animal form.'

'I think the owners will be just as

intrigued,' Adam remarked, looking at Elissa. 'Possibly it will even encourage them to lose weight too if they've a problem — like Mrs Preston and Lavender, for instance.'

Elissa had her doubts about Mrs Preston! But all the same she smiled. 'I've a class for tomorrow afternoon. Everyone I contacted was able to come, so I thought I would begin with weighing and then a brief outline of the average energy needs of adult dogs, followed by constructing individual diet-sheets for each patient.'

'What a brilliant idea!' Barbara exclaimed. 'I'm sure it will be a tremendous success.'

'Perhaps you'd like to join us and see for yourself?' Elissa suggested.

'I'd love to. Could I bring Blimp?'

Elissa grinned. 'Only if he's prepared to act as a model! I'm going to include a few grooming hints too, and Blimp seems very good-natured ... Do you think he'd pose?'

Everyone laughed, and Blimp wagged

his stumpy tail as though he understood what had been said. Elissa was
suddenly aware of Adam's gaze as he
sat on the lounger, dressed in a dark
blue shirt and jaunty red tie, his elegant
dark trousers showing the firm muscled
outline of his long legs. He looked very
relaxed, and for a moment his eyes held
hers. Their expression took her breath
away, as, wishing her heart would stop
racing, she tried to concentrate on what
Barbara was saying.

When Sharon called them for waiting
clients and Barbara drove away in her
little car with Blimp on the back shelf,
Elissa made mental notes: first, to
cancel the advertisement for a nurse,
for Barbara had agreed tentatively to
take the job; second, to spend the
evening looking through her dietary
management notes and preparing for
tomorrow. She had no booked appointments for the afternoon, leaving the
way clear for the weight-watching
session, and now she was beginning to
feel really excited about the project.

Late in the afternoon, Adam stopped by her room. 'I've phoned the Birmingham hospital,' he called to her. 'Mr Martin's quite comfortable, but as I wasn't a relative they wouldn't say more.'

Elissa nodded. 'At least it's over for him.' Her jaw dropped suddenly. 'Oh dear, talking of Mr Martin and his operation has reminded me of someone else who is sick. Gwen Richards. I was intending to look in and see if there was anything I could do to help. She had such a dreadful cough last time I saw her.'

'Gwen Richards at Vale Farm?' Adam nodded thoughtfully. 'I've a call to make at another farm not far away. Why don't we go in my car?'

Elissa hesitated. 'But that leaves the surgery unmanned.'

'Sharon will stay until we return. Surgery is over for the day. Anything vital, she can ring us through on the car phone.'

'Well . . . I suppose the two calls are close . . . '

179

'We'd better get moving,' Adam suggested swiftly. 'It looks like a thunderstorm overhead if I'm not much mistaken.'

The first spots of summer rain fell as they hurried to the Mercedes. He slid in beside her, his blue shirt spotted with wet patches, his black hair falling over his face. She tossed back her auburn waves from her eyes, her eyelashes blinking off the drops. A fresh curtain of water swept hectically across the windscreen, obliterating everything from view.

'I love these changes in weather,' Elissa gasped, excitedly shivering under her cotton blouse which moulded damply to her body. 'No other place is quite like England in the rain!'

Adam laughed as he started the engine. 'A glutton for punishment, eh?' He ran his gaze over her, his dark eyes making her skin tingle with their intensity. 'Do you want to go back for wet-gear?'

For a moment she stared back at him, the sensation of his warm body next to her, and his dark eyes, making her colour deepen and her throat dry. 'N . . . no,' she stammered, stiffening back into her seat. 'It's just a shower, that's all.'

Quickly he turned his attention to the road and, putting the car into gear, he pulled out of the drive and for a while they drove in silence.

'The cow is on a course of antibiotics, you mentioned?' he asked at length, squinting through the backlash of water from the wipers.

Elissa nodded as she glued her eyes to the road. 'I'm mostly concerned about what will happen when Maddy goes. Gwen will have no one. The farm's being sold. Both her husband and son died, the remaining son she hasn't heard of for some years. Apart from her immediate neighbours, she has no one.'

'Social services? Her church? Surely she must have someone?'

Elissa shook her head. 'Not according to what Dad told me at Easter. She's almost a recluse at Vale Farm. No help.

No friends. I don't know what the social services could do. I suppose they would be a last resort after the farm was sold.'

Adam remained silent as a bolt of lightning veered across the purple-blue sky, illuminating the darkening landscape, the deluge running in deep sandy ruts in the muddy lane which approached Vale Farm.

The place looked more dismal than ever when they drove up and Elissa noticed water pouring from the leaking gutters, while there was no obvious sign of life in the house.

'Something's wrong!' Her heart raced suddenly.

Adam brought the car to a halt. 'Here, put this on.' He swung an arm over to the back and hauled a cagoule over the seat, but Elissa was too concerned to bother with it.

Luckily the rain eased briefly as they ran to the house, but though the door was open and they were able to enter, there was no warmth, no light and no movement as they searched the darkened rooms.

'Upstairs?' Adam said softly. Together they trod the carpetless flight until, in one of the small, damp-smelling bedrooms, they discovered Gwen lying on a bed.

Elissa rushed forward. 'Whatever's happened, Gwen?'

Adam was there beside her and leant across, unsnapping his case, pulling out his stethoscope to examine Gwen's chest as she coughed violently. He glanced at Elissa. 'Bronchitis.'

Elissa clutched the small, fevered hand. 'Gwen, can you talk? How long have you been here, like this?'

'Since yesterday,' came the whispered reply.

'And Maddy?' Elissa asked, her heart sinking.

Gwen's eyes filled with tears.

Elissa guessed what had happened. The old woman said nothing, but cried quietly to herself, the tears falling down her cheeks.

Adam drew Elissa aside. 'We must get her to hospital. I'm going to carry her to the car. Could you bring any pills you can find, maybe a dressing-gown and slippers and a night-dress? And those sticks on the floor too.'

Elissa nodded. 'Adam, I feel dreadful for not coming before. She had the most awful cough when I visited her earlier in the week. I should have known.'

He squeezed both her cold hands in his. 'How could you? Don't be silly! We've arrived in time, that's the important thing.'

He walked back to the bed to wrap Gwen's small frame in the blanket. Linking his hands under her, he pulled her up and against his broad chest.

He had already settled her on the back seat when Elissa dashed to the car with the few belongings she could find, the rain soaking her hair and dripping down her thin blouse.

He glanced up, his shirt soaked too as he pulled a blanket from the boot.

'Quickly, get in the dry. Where was Maddy when you last saw her?'

'In the shed behind the house. I'd better check,' Elissa said, and then, as she went to go, he restrained her and shook his head.

'I'll go. You make Gwen comfortable with this blanket.'

Five minutes later he was back, climbing into the driving seat, raindrops steering an erratic path down his brown cheeks. He brushed them away with the crook of his arm, flicking a solemn glance at her.

He made two brief calls on the mobile phone, one to Elissa's god-father, who agreed to make the visit to the other farm on Adam's behalf, and another to Sharon at the surgery. Then, glancing with a reassuring smile at Elissa, he reached into the back seat to take Gwen's arthritic hand. 'We'll get you into Farwell hospital, Gwen. Then I shall make arrangements for Maddy. Don't worry. Elissa and I will do all that's necessary.'

Elissa focused back on the windscreen.

His kindness touched her so deeply that a lump formed in her throat. As they drove she found a fresh ache springing up inside her which made her only too well aware of how her relationship with Adam was changing. Her feelings, she realised, were beginning to rule her heart and were dangerously close to ruling her head.

7

Casualty at Farwell Cottage Hospital was not busy, fortunately, and before long Gwen was seen and admitted to a ward.

Adam brought two cups of strong coffee as they stopped to catch their breath in the waiting-room. 'Don't worry,' he smiled, turning the polystyrene mug between his fingers. 'Gwen will be OK. Another day or two and she might not have been, though. Because you decided to check on her, you've probably saved her life.'

Elissa relaxed back in her chair, feeling very guilty that she had not remembered to call at Gwen's before, but Adam's words were comforting all the same.

She looked up at him with a weak smile. 'Thank you for your help today.'

He nodded. 'I'll drive you home

now.' Abruptly he moved to throw his unfinished coffee into the waste-paper bin.

As they drove out of the hospital car park, Elissa sighed, feeling the energy drain out of her. After a vague effort at conversation they drove in silence through the wet lanes, a fine drizzle replacing the earlier thunderstorm.

At Larkhill, the perfume of honeysuckle was potent in the rainy air as Adam opened the front door. 'I'll lock up the surgery and drive Sharon home. It's rather late for her to be catching a bus. It will only take five minutes, meanwhile I'll switch the phones through. Why don't you make yourself something to eat?'

'But what about you? You must be ravenous.' Elissa wondered if his guests were upstairs waiting for him, though she had seen no white Porsche parked outside or lights in the house.

He shrugged unenthusiastically. 'Not really. As a matter of fact I'll try to contact the authorities when I come back. Gwen's cow has been dead for more than twenty-four hours and they'll have to fumigate the place.'

She looked up sharply. 'Oh, poor Gwen!'

'Yes, she must have been extremely upset.' He smiled softly. 'Try not to worry. See you in the morning. Goodnight, Elissa.'

He went, with broad shoulders slightly hunched, taking long strides, towards the connecting door, Arnie following him.

When he was gone Elissa realised she was very tired; she had even gone past the need to eat. Glancing at the stairs, she wished she had had more time to talk to Adam tonight. But what was she thinking? She must be very tired, for of course it was not her company he desired, but Minty's.

Sleep was virtually impossible, though the day had been long. Her mind strayed repeatedly to Vale Farm and the discovery of Gwen and how Adam had attended to her with such compassion.

However, she finally awoke to a radiant morning. Sun poured in through the French windows as she phoned the hospital before her open surgery at nine. Gwen's condition was stable and, a little comforted, Elissa went to find Adam. To her surprise, he had not yet gone into surgery but came in through the front door of Larkhill.

'Good morning!' His dark hair swept back from his face and he was dressed in a crisp white working shirt. 'Have you phoned the hospital yet?' he asked immediately.

After she explained, he nodded. 'I'm sure she'll improve. Oh, yes, I alerted the authorities and the farm has been taken care of, so perhaps when Gwen is feeling better we can call to see her and reassure her.'

Elissa glanced past him to the open front door, as it swung on its hinges, nudged by the light summer breeze wafting through the house.

Adam followed her gaze. 'Er — Minty and Philip have gone. Some unexpected business cropped up apparently and they had to return to London. They asked me to say goodbye and to thank you for Larkhill's hospitality.'

Elissa did not answer as a wave of relief engulfed her, promptly followed by an avalanche of guilt. Struggling with an impulse to let out a deep sigh, she found herself walking with Adam to the surgery, unable to believe that it was Minty's sudden absence which brought such a lightened feel to the beginning of her day.

After lunch, Elissa discovered the surgery hectic with dogs. Sharon ushered them in to Reception as Barbara hurried to meet Elissa. 'Can I help?' she asked excitedly, clutching Blimp under one arm. 'Adam suggested the garden. I suppose it is rather a good idea.'

Elissa raised uncertain eyebrows. 'Yes, the weather is fine enough, I suppose.'

Mrs Preston heaved a portly Lavender over the threshold, interrupting. 'I thought the day would never dawn. I'm so excited,' she giggled, and tugged Lavender off to sniff another kindred spirit.

Barbara laughed. 'This is going to be

fun!' She lowered Blimp to the floor, where with typical Jack Russell gusto he bared his teeth at the heavyweights towering above him. 'Adam's put chairs out for us,' Barbara explained. 'But of course the scales will have to stay in here. What would you like me to do?'

Elissa had decided to take the class in her consulting-room or Reception, depending on how many turned up, but the garden idea on such a lovely day she thought a good one, especially since the class appeared to be instantly popular.

'I'll take a roll-call in Reception, Barbara,' Elissa decided swiftly. 'If you will weigh each dog on the scales and then point them towards the garden, I'll take all my notes out with me too.'

Adam strolled in. 'Need any help?'

Elissa shook her head, smiling. 'Thanks for putting the chairs in the garden.'

He left with a rueful smile as the last client, with her retriever, hurried into Reception to take a seat.

'Lavender!' Elissa called, deciding that she might as well begin with her biggest worry, and Mrs Preston flustered across the room, tugging a sluggish Lavender after her.

The woman collapsed into a nearby chair with a sigh. 'I'm at the end of my tether,' she explained, as her audience fell silent. 'I've been up every night since I last saw Miss Hart — Lavender doesn't suffer in silence, you know, and she misses her treats.' She paused to an accompanying nod of heads. 'And then when I'm up, I make myself a milky drink to get me back off to sleep and then . . . Well, I'm hungry all of a sudden and so is she. I just can't resist giving her a snack, hoping she'll go off too.'

Again, Elissa noticed, the other women appeared to be sympathetic. She took a deep breath and began. 'It's difficult, I know, especially at first when a new eating regime is implemented. Lavender is probably beginning to expect a midnight feast every night. So you must try to break the habit, which will, with Lavender's appetite and expectations, only become more entrenched.'

'It's easy enough to say,' Mrs Preston grumbled to everyone. 'You see, I sympathise with Lavender. I love my food and I can't bear to see her go hungry. I've tried dozens of times to lose weight, but I can't. I'm really getting very depressed about it all.'

Elissa could see that the situation was getting out of hand, both for patient and client. 'Did you write down everything Lavender has eaten?' she asked above the murmurings.

Mrs Preston proudly produced a list. 'Every crumb!'

Barbara smiled wryly as she persuaded Lavender off the scales. 'Forty-six kilograms,' she sighed.

The room gave an audible mutter.

'Twelve kilograms too heavy,' Elissa explained, but then laughed lightly. 'If she were a bull mastiff, she'd be just the right weight!'

Everyone laughed and the tension eased. 'Next week,' Elissa explained to Mrs Preston, 'if you keep to the diet-sheet I give you, Lavender may well have lost two or three kilograms. It doesn't seem much, but it is a beginning. Substitute the midnight feasts by going on a couple of short walks around the garden — you should find Lavender will settle.' Elissa wasn't so sure the same could be said for Mrs Preston, by the twinkle in her eye, but perhaps if she could convince her of the sensible use of protein, fat and carbohydrates in her own diet, and a restriction of sugar, a miracle might happen.

When all the dogs were weighed, the gathering moved to the garden where Adam had placed chairs in a semicircle on the lawn. Thoughtfully he had stacked a trolley with tins of special dietary food.

When all was quiet, Elissa handed out practical written feeding hints. 'Each dog's energy requirements depend on the body-size and age as well as the lifestyle of the individual animal,' she explained carefully. 'Big dogs have a smaller energy requirement per unit of body-weight than small ones. Adults within a breed have smaller energy needs per unit of body-weight than their puppies. In other words, contrary to popular belief, a sixty-five kilogram Newfoundland doesn't need five times as much food as a fourteen-kilogram beagle!'

'Does that mean I don't need more food because I'm taller?' asked one woman doubtfully. 'I always thought I had more space to fill.'

Elissa shook her head to the murmur of amusement. 'If you take enough exercise you'll burn off any extra weight you might put on, whatever your height, but it certainly won't help if you come back from a walk and eat a pastry before your meal in the evening.'

'I'm big-boned,' another put in. 'And so is my dog,' she added, pointing to her plump retriever. 'Naturally we're fatter.'

Elissa patiently considered the dog's weight reading. 'She's too heavy by eight kilograms at least. Whether she has big bones or not doesn't really come into it; her ideal weight should be thirty-two kilograms.'

'I can't be bothered counting calories for myself, let alone Rosie!' exclaimed a portly woman with a very fat cocker spaniel.

'Then this special canned pet food will be of great value to you,' Elissa suggested. 'It's a scientifically concentrated food with minerals and vitamins added to ensure she stays in peak condition. It is possible to prepare food for your dog, but it's difficult to get the nutrients right. This food will be very good for Lavender too, Mrs Preston. We'll try her on one and a half tins of this per day with a handful of wholemeal mixer biscuits, a little for breakfast and the rest for an evening meal.'

'I wish it was as easy for me!' Mrs Preston exclaimed.

Elissa paused. 'There are some specially prepared calorie-counted foods for humans too — why don't you invest in some of them for the freezer and lose weight with Lavender?'

Looking not altogether impressed with the suggestion, Mrs Preston heaved her shoulders on a sigh.

Realising it was time for a little light

relief, Elissa asked Barbara to hold Blimp while she demonstrated how to check his ears. He stood staunchly, allowing her to fold back the silky flaps and test them with the soft pad of her fingers for alien irritants. As she ruffled his coat backwards and parted the frown on his forehead to search for the presence of fleas, the class followed her example with their own dogs. When this was over, Elissa decided on a cup of tea, and left the group to sit in the warm sunshine while she and Barbara collected trays from a forewarned Grace.

'Is there a spare cup going?' Adam asked, strolling into the garden.

'Of course!' Elissa poured him one.

'How did it go?' he asked with a rueful smile.

She nodded. 'Very well, actually. But I have my doubts as to whether my star pupil will respond to her diet.'

'Oh, the redoubtable Lavender?' Adam grinned, glancing at the Labrador sniffing at the trays on the patio table for crumbs.

'No,' Elissa laughed lightly. 'Mrs Preston! I've suggested she diet with Lavender too, but I don't think the idea went down too well.'

Adam was amused. 'I'll circulate. Perhaps I can offer her a little encouragement.'

Elissa watched him as she drank her tea, noticing the way her clients responded to him as, with bent head, he listened to their problems, occasionally glancing back to her with a grin. It was her undoing, she realised with a jerk of her heart; he caused the unbidden sensations inside her to flare, those which she tried to ignore, but which manifested themselves without rhyme or reason.

She took a moment to steady herself, drinking her tea. Someone came up and began talking, and vaguely she responded, aware of Adam's movements all the time, his tall, broad-shouldered figure and dark hair, always on the periphery of her vision, just as, it seemed, he was of her life.

Suddenly she realised that he was having trouble in disengaging himself from his admirers and, as he looked across the bobbing heads and raised dark eyebrows, she headed towards the tight little group around him in answer to his silent call.

'I'm sorry to interrupt,' she smiled apologetically, 'but I think it's time I gave everyone their diet-sheets. Shall we go into Reception?'

Adam gave her a grateful, intimate smile. She grinned in return, lowering her eyes as her skin grew warm, hoping neither he nor her clients could hear the rapid thudding of her heart which seemed, ridiculously, to be deafening her.

Later, when all was quiet and Sharon had locked the front door and hurried out to meet her boyfriend, who met her most evenings from work, Elissa turned to discover Adam watching her as he stood on the threshold of her consulting-room.

'The decorators want to begin in here tomorrow,' he said, studying the ceiling and walls. 'You can use the spare consulting-room — or mine if you wish . . . '

She smiled, sensing a change in the atmosphere, very slight, but one which caused her pulse to speed, alarming her as she swallowed. 'No, the spare room will be fine, thanks.'

He nodded, seeming hesitant to go. Finally, he said, 'It's been a busy day. I wonder . . . Would you like to eat in Farwell? I'm sure Grace wouldn't be offended if we treated ourselves to some supper out.'

Elissa thought wryly that there was no way in which this could be an offer of a foursome!

'You're smiling. Have I said something funny?' he asked, with a curious frown.

Elissa quickly shook her head as a thought struck her. 'Better still, since we would have to switch our calls through to Harry's practice, why don't I make supper here? I'm sure Grace's stockpile runs to pasta or omelettes . . . if you're not terribly bothered about what I might concoct?'

He laughed too. 'I'd like that.'

Elissa wondered why she was already planning a more appealing setting than the kitchen in which to eat and why, once again, the rapid run of her pulse was galloping ahead, beyond her normal control.

★ ★ ★

That evening, she tried on a black velour top and a skirt of glittery gold which was far too frivolous, discarding them for a red and white spotted chiffon blouse and black culottes, which seemed not much better. Throwing these on to the bed, she sank with a sigh, clad only in white panties and bra, into the middle of the unsuitable pile.

She wondered why she had made the suggestion of eating at home in the first place if she was going to get so flustered about it. Probably eating out would have been more sensible in the long run.

Elissa reached into the wardrobe. Last-ditch effort, she thought, glancing at her watch. She pulled out her hand-woven African dress, her coming-home outfit. The colour of the simple linen shift was the colour of her hair. Without sleeves, the shape hugged her slim curves, the split on the side just reaching up to her thigh to make an otherwise plain cut into a stunning one.

Having decided that the dress was appropriate, she opened the door to Adam at a little after nine. He stood hesitantly, his dark eyes studying her, moving over her slowly. Then, pushing a bottle wrapped in blue tissue paper into her hands, he smiled and said swiftly, 'I thought this might come in useful with . . . whatever it is that smells so delicious!'

She smiled, examining the label as they walked through the hall into the drawing-room. 'Goodness, champagne!'

'Why not?' He shrugged. 'After all, your day was a positive success.'

'You mean the weight-watching class?' She grinned ruefully. 'Yes, it was rather, wasn't it? All those who attended today are coming next week too. I think they are all coming just to see if Mrs Preston has lost any weight, let alone Lavender!'

They both laughed, but, as a purple and yellow sunset broke in waves across the dying sky and reflected its last rays into the room, they fell into silence. She stood self-consciously, aware of his gaze. He was dressed in a black polo shirt and black trousers, and her anxious heart seemed to dither as she tried hard to concentrate on what she had prepared to eat.

She led him into the dining-room, furnished with the Georgian table and chairs belonging to her grandparents. Setting the table, she had thought of all the generations who had eaten at it. Now she was about to entertain her first guest, who until recently had been a complete stranger.

'Shall I light the candles?' Adam noticed the silver candelabra she had placed in the middle of the table, not really for use but as decoration.

However, she nodded, feeling strangely light-headed as she watched him apply a match to the wick of each twisted green candle. The room glowed with a delicate light, and long, flickering shadows were cast across the polished wood of the table.

The consommé followed by scampi and thermidor sauce was an unqualified success. They talked as they ate, finally devouring the tiny caramels topped with butterscotch. Adam told her of his mother, who had died while he was in the States, and of his father's referral practice in London. She was surprised to learn he had an older brother too, a journalist in Canada.

Of the years Adam himself spent abroad, Elissa read between the lines. He had worked in a sophisticated Los Angeles practice, and made her laugh with humorous anecdotes of over-pampered and often humanised companion animals. But she realised it must have been quite a glamorous lifestyle all the same.

'Life in California sounds exciting,'

Elissa remarked, as she had time to study his strong, chiselled features enhanced by the unreal light.

He leaned his forearms on the table, giving her a vague smile. 'Yes, I suppose you could say it was. I gave myself five years, after taking my consultant's certificate in England, to travel and gain experience, but I always knew I would return to Britain.'

Elissa ran her finger around the rim of her glass thoughtfully, her long lashes flicking down on to her cheeks as she wondered if he would refer to his engagement to Minty. But he said nothing more as he rested back in the carver's chair, the one her father had always used. Elissa's heart gave a little twist. But she was not unhappy this time, as she had been on the first day they had met, when Adam had worn her father's greens in Theatre.

She dragged her eyes away from his gaze and shifted her chair from the table. 'Coffee in the drawing-room?'

He lifted his head as she rose,

watching her as she began to remove the plates. 'Let me help.'

She shook her head. 'No. I'm pretty well-organised. The kitchen in this flat is quite small,' she heard herself protesting lamely, not wanting to be in such a confined space with him. 'Make yourself comfortable. I shan't be long with the coffee.'

Escaping to the kitchen, she stacked the dishes to one side, taking a breath, expanding her lungs. As she poured coffee from the percolator, her fingers misbehaved and tipped the cream over the edge of the small jug, which she wiped and placed unsteadily on the tray.

'I asked Barbara to ring in the morning,' she said brightly as she went back into the drawing-room, placing the tray on the table and pouring two cups of coffee. 'To confirm her starting part-time with us.'

He nodded. 'I'm glad you liked her.'

Elissa sat down on the sofa beside him, for it would be too noticeable if she took the far chair. She watched him stir his coffee slowly with strong, brown fingers.

She sat very still, concentrating on her cup. Suddenly he lowered his to the coffee-table and reached across to remove hers from her tightly clenched fingers. Then he slid his fingers slowly into her hair, their tips playing with the curls which fell around her ears.

'Elissa . . . ' he whispered, and tilted up her chin towards him, 'I've been wanting to do this all evening . . . ' As he bent to kiss her, her body seemed to melt and she arched towards him, her hands sliding involuntarily along the curve of his shoulders and into his thick hair. Soon nothing else in the world existed. His kiss deepened and she began to match his exploration of her mouth with equal excitement and intensity, hardly aware of his hand running down to the slender jut of her hip, caressing it smoothly, sliding down to her thigh.

'You're so lovely, Elissa,' he muttered

hoarsely as he pulled her close, his kisses covering the throbbing pulse in her neck as he buried his face in her hair, whispering so softly that she could not hear him, her own heart throbbing with desire as heat seemed to engulf them.

His fingers came down to press open the tiny raffia buttons of her dress, smoothing open the V to stroke her breasts, which were now tensed and tingling, covered only flimsily by the white silk of her camisole. Flushed, with a wave of weakness flooding through her, wanting him so much, she pushed her hands against his chest, staring up into the heavy-lidded dark eyes.

'The phone . . . I think,' she mumbled, straining her ears for the insistent sound coming from somewhere in the house.

With a quiet oath he moved. 'I'll go,' he murmured huskily, kissing her again briefly on the lips, his smile soft.

She heard his footfall along the passage to the door which led out into the main hall, wondering why the phone was ringing so distantly, suddenly remembering that she had meant to switch it through and had forgotten in the rush earlier this evening.

Moments seemed to slip by as she sank back into the sofa, his face imprinted on her mind, the way his lips had felt, the movement of his hands over her body. She shook her head to clear the memory, then rose, wandering along the passage.

Was it an emergency call? A road accident? Elissa arrived in the hall, but Adam had his back to her, talking in subdued tones. 'I can't,' she heard. 'You know it's impossible for me to leave.'

Then a pause. Elissa watched him, the strong back, the broad shoulders over which her hands had travelled.

'Minty, listen to me. I can't leave Larkhill at the moment, you will have to come here.'

Another longer pause, as Elissa stared mesmerised at the black polo shirt.

'Yes, that's fine. But can't you

persuade Philip not to come? I'd prefer to see you alone.'

Elissa turned, walked back down the passageway, went into the drawing-room and threw open the French windows, and walked into the garden and the warm night. She did not know how long she stood there before Adam came up behind her and took her into his arms.

'You're trembling,' he whispered, gazing down at her.

'Am I?' She stiffened, glad she could not see his face in the darkness. She forbade herself to make a scene, telling herself to keep composed. The shock she had received was like a physical blow, seeming to hit her straight in the stomach, dispelling all the desire which he had brought to such a peak back there in the drawing-room. Still, there was too much at stake to lose over one reckless mistake which she had obviously made.

'Would you rather I went?' he asked, sensing her change of mood, sliding his hands down her bare, chilled arms.

She nodded, unable to speak for the moment, withdrawing from him.

'Elissa . . . what's wrong?'

There was a long and, for Elissa, painful silence. He made no reference to the call. He didn't even say who it was. And she wasn't going to ask. She'd heard enough.

'Elissa?'

'I'm feeling rather tired and it is late,' she said unsteadily, thinking for one moment that he was going to protest. 'Goodnight, Adam.'

Her heart slammed achingly against her chest. But after a while he turned silently, going in through the French windows, a tall silhouette against the spear of light coming from the drawing-room.

She waited until he had gone. For a few seconds she stood in the garden, wondering how she could possibly have allowed herself to make such a dreadful mistake with Adam Kennedy.

She had heard with her own ears his

suggestion of dispensing with Philip Saville, and there was no mistaking his disappointment at Minty's refusal. Yet only minutes before he had been about to make love to her.

Elissa remembered the way he had made her feel, the way she had wanted him, forgetting entirely the presence of Minty in his life — wanting to forget! He had obliterated every thought from her mind, the sensation of his lovemaking overwhelming her. Her lips, her skin, her body had responded as though she had wanted him from the first moment he had walked into her life.

8

Before morning surgery Adam walked in to her consulting-room. He looked tall and lean and very dark-eyed. 'How are you feeling this morning?' he asked, almost scornfully.

Elissa shrugged. 'Well enough, thank you.'

'I suppose it's no good asking you what happened last night?' Not giving her time to answer, he went on, 'I take it I'm not allowed to know the reason why you completely withdrew from me — other than feeling tired, of course?'

Elissa could hardly believe he was asking her that. Was he really the kind of man who enjoyed forays into relationships with several women at one time, or had the experience with Minty and their broken engagement made him bitter?

'I don't think this is going to get us

anywhere,' Elissa answered, as her cheeks grew red. 'We'll end up quarrelling and it won't do either of us any good. We haven't exactly seen eye to eye professionally, let alone allowing personal conflict to come between us.'

He studied her for a long time, his mouth finally showing white as he closed his lips together tightly. 'By that I take it you're not happy with our partnership?'

'I didn't say that — '

'Well, what else am I expected to believe?' he interrupted angrily, drawing back his shoulders. 'I simply don't understand what's going on. Every time you and I — '

'You see?' Elissa shook her head. 'We've started already and the day hasn't even begun yet. Adam, please let's leave the subject alone!'

A muscle in his jaw twitched as he pulled himself upright. 'Does this mean you won't be assisting me in Theatre today?'

She gasped in exasperation. 'Of

course it doesn't! Sharon has left me free time this morning to help you.' She walked to the door. 'What time would you like me to come along?'

He shrugged, his face tense still. 'I've just administered the prep to Breeze. About ten o'clock.'

With this settled, he walked past her into the hall, almost colliding with Barbara. She heard his deep voice in brief conversation for a few minutes, and then listened in relief as he walked away.

Well, she told herself, it was over, the moment she had been dreading. An all-out argument between them had been avoided, and no doubt a dozen excuses on Adam's part regarding the phone call if she had tackled him about it. It would, in retrospect, have been crushingly embarrassing to admit she had listened to the conversation, even more so to reveal her hurt feelings.

Elissa went through some of the ideas she had with Barbara. It wasn't easy at first, since her body was still in a state of anxiety, the rush of angry blood still winging its way through her veins. Sharing in Barbara's infectious enthusiasm, she was able to channel her thoughts in another direction for a few precious moments, so that when Barbara left, she felt reasonably calm. However, there was no escaping the fact, in the light of what she now knew, that she would have to make unavoidable changes to her life if Minty and Adam decided to marry.

Realising that it was almost ten, she scrubbed up and walked to Adam's unit, trying to put the question out of her mind. He sat at the microscope dressed in his greens. Breeze lay on the operating table in front of him, a self-adhesive sterile drape over her head and upper body.

'The machine just behind you,' he explained briskly, without looking at her as she stood beside him, 'is linked to the microscope through ultra-sound, as you know. Basically, it's designed to atomise the lens on the eye and aspirate with fluid.'

Elissa watched as he gestured to the pedals beneath his feet. 'There's a double foot-pedal for the microscope and a treble for the machine. I work them independently, rather like a sewing-machine. You can see my movements up there on the video screen.'

Focusing on Breeze and the anaesthetic machine, Elissa checked the dog's pulse and respiration, making sure they were normal. Adam cast her a swift glance, but very soon he lent his eye to the microscope and was lost in his work.

Using a disposable speculum to hold the eyelids apart, Elissa watched him insert a minute plastic drape over the bottom lid to move the eyelashes out of the way. 'It's important to keep a perfectly sterile situation as I clear the optic pathway,' he explained. 'Here you can see the bottom eyelid and the third eyelid, with some little plasma cell infiltrations.'

Now he showed her how to operate the machine and Elissa copied his movements to his satisfied nod. She watched the picture on the video screen revealing what was hidden from the naked eye as fluid went into the cornea from the tool Adam was using. He then snipped the side of the eyelid so that he could work freely, anchoring the eye with sutures finer than human hair.

The minuscule incision of the lens was made with a diamond knife and the matter underneath drawn out with forceps. It was a delicate procedure which demanded deep concentration, and for a while Elissa forgot about everything except the skill of Adam's fingers.

'Now the lens is removed I'll put in a single suture,' he said at last, removing the tiny sterile drape which had played such an important part in keeping the eye perfectly clean. He relaxed his broad shoulders. 'All done!'

Elissa began to dispense with the sterile cloths, thinking that the forty minutes which had passed seemed like only four. Fitting Breeze to the drip, she realised that she had been so impressed by the operation that she had lost track of time. 'Do you think the sight in that eye will be fully restored?' she asked, as they lifted the dog into a warm recovery cage.

'I can't see any reason why not.' Adam watched Breeze for a few seconds, then smiled. 'She's a game little collie. I think Mr McKenna will be pleasantly surprised.'

Elissa sighed. 'I was totally lost as I watched you. It was wonderful.'

'Technology,' Adam said modestly. 'But for machines like this, we'd all still be back in the Dark Ages.'

She understood suddenly what a hopeless position she was in for, despite what she had overheard last night and how angry she had been, she still couldn't stop the heightened awareness she felt in his presence or the lurching of her heart when she gazed into those beautiful dark eyes. She drew a deep breath, trying to think practically.

'I'd better get back to Sharon and see

who we have waiting in surgery.'

He linked his fingers around her arm as she went to move. 'Don't go for a moment. Elissa — '

A polite smile pinned to her lips, she moved her arm from his grasp. 'Let's not go over it, Adam. I hope we understand one another.'

'I thought we did,' he answered her shortly. 'Are you telling me I made a mistake when I kissed you?'

Elissa looked away to compose herself, an anguish in her heart she couldn't understand. 'I think you know the answer to that, Adam,' she returned swiftly.

'There's someone else?' His face was tense, his eyes fixed on her, his voice husky. 'Is it Philip?'

'Philip?' Elissa frowned. What had Philip to do with this? Then comprehension suddenly dawned as Adam lifted his broad shoulders, looking at her accusingly.

'You two got on extremely well. He's an attractive man . . . and you're a very lovely young woman. It's natural I should draw the conclusion, especially if — '

'Especially if I refused to let you make love to me last night?' she retorted angrily.

A darkness flushed his face as she took a painful breath, realising he was trying to shift the blame to Philip, his jealousy of the man obviously very near to the surface.

'Then we both know where we stand,' he said before she could speak. He shrugged, turning away from her. 'I'm going to stay with Breeze. You might as well go and have some lunch while it's quiet.' And with that he was gone, leaving the door to swing on its hinges, leaving Elissa speechless.

★　★　★

During the afternoon, the Cavalier King Charles arrived. Elissa decided that if Adam wanted help he could ask for it. As Barbara had come in to help during the morning, autoclaving some of the instruments in the laundry-room and doing a stock-check of drugs and sterile cloths, the afternoon was free for Sharon to take bookings and for Elissa to take open surgery.

Just as Elissa was wondering if the lull between patients was temporary and trying very hard not to let her mind wander to earlier events, the intercom buzzed on her desk.

'Would you like to come in and give me some help with the Cavalier King Charles?' Adam said crisply. 'If you're not busy, of course.'

She could hardly say she was, and besides, resorting to childish behaviour was hardly going to resolve anything. She discovered Adam clasping the Cavalier King Charles, who was shaking badly.

'Where is the owner?' Elissa asked as she looked round the room.

'Sharon took her to Reception for a cup of tea. She's very distraught, both with the dog's reaction and his wet face, which has become worse.'

Elissa nodded, gently taking hold of the dog. 'What's his name?'

'Charles, would you believe?' Adam began to fill a syringe. 'I'm going to give him a tranquilliser or I shall never be able to get near the eyes. I need to know if there is real pain or whether it's just a plumbing problem, in which case, in view of his age, I wouldn't operate.'

Several minutes later, as Elissa smoothed the silky white coat, she began to feel the uncoiling of tense muscles beneath her fingertips. Suddenly Adam's hand touched hers as his strong brown fingers slipped down over the dog's coat, examining the selfsame muscles.

Elissa felt herself jump as she quickly pulled away. 'Would you like the room darkened and the headlight put on?' she asked, keeping her face expressionless, or at least she hoped so.

Adam nodded. She went to draw the blinds and switch on the powerful ophthalmic headlight set which incorporated magnifying lenses. Fortunately the bright light had a hypnotic effect on Charles and he lay on his side, panting a little, but relaxed enough for Adam to examine his eyes.

As Elissa spread a sterile sheet over the dog, she watched Adam position his ophthalmoscope. The instrument was based on a torch, with small lenses able to be moved into a small aperture in the eyepiece, and with it he could, at last, examine all the eye structures. Finally, dimming the light, he measured the eyes with a tonometer, so gauging the pressure inside the eyeball.

'No glaucoma present,' he said with relief, 'but the treatment of the drops hasn't made very much difference either. The nasolacrimal duct appears to be healthy,' he added, using a pen torch to examine the interior of Charles's nose. 'Otherwise I might have considered an operation to divert saliva from the mouth to the cornea.'

Elissa nodded. 'What is really Charles's problem, do you think?'

Adam straightened his back. 'Epiphora,

I feel. The profuse nasal drainage of tears from the eyes is making a considerable wet face. But Charles is eight and, though epiphora is a nuisance, a new eye medication which has recently come on the market will alleviate the wetness to some extent. But he'll have to have an Elizabethan collar for the first week, because he's been irritating his eyes by bringing up his back leg and scratching.'

'And you'll want to see him again?'

Adam nodded slowly. 'While Charles is recovering, I'll have a chat with his owner and try to persuade her into the merits of having a rather cumbersome and inelegant plastic collar fitted around her pet's neck.'

Some time later Elissa walked with Charles and his new plastic collar into Reception. The owner looked as though she did not know whether to laugh or cry, but accepted the lead, and Adam walked with them to the car, talking in the way he had of reassuring people.

Several patients now waited in open

226

surgery. These were straightforward, one a young dog needing worming, the others booster vaccinations, and Elissa saw to them, relieved that the first two referral cases appeared to have gone without a hitch.

At the close of the day, Breeze was well into recovery. Adam had covered the eye with gauze after examining it, and was just tempting Breeze with a little scrambled egg when Elissa walked into the recovery-room. He looked up and smiled. 'She's coming along well. I think we'll keep her with us until the weekend, make sure she's clear of any infection before she goes home.'

Elissa nodded, admiring his conscientious attitude. There was so much about him she did admire that it was hard to believe his attitude towards women. Despite all her defences, he had become important to her in a way no other man ever had, only for her to realise that he was in love with Minty . . . And still that realisation made no difference to the way she felt, no matter what she told herself.

'Goodnight, Adam,' she called softly and, without waiting for a reply, hurried out of the surgery to the house.

*   *   *

As though Adam recognised her desire to be left alone, Elissa found she rarely bumped into him over the next few days. The longest time they spoke was to relay a conversation she had with the Briard's owner, who was unable to attend the referral appointment and asked to make another.

The weekend arrived and there was no sudden deluge of visitors either. Elissa felt herself able to breathe a small sigh of relief. Not that the weekend was over yet, she told herself with due caution.

She was further surprised when, on calling in to the surgery on Saturday morning as Mr McKenna came in to collect Breeze, Adam asked her to wait before leaving.

'She's looking as fit as a fiddle!' Mr McKenna bent to stroke Breeze as she sat quietly at his feet.

'Yes, she is,' Adam agreed. 'The operation successfully removed the cataract. I'd like you to bring her in next week when I'll check her again. Until then, just make sure she doesn't scratch or roll in dirt or allow anything alien to enter her eye.'

Mr McKenna nodded. 'I'll make sure! See you next week and thanks a lot, Mr Kennedy.'

Adam saw him out, then returned to Elissa. As it was not her duty morning she was wearing a sleeveless summer frock of small purple-pink flowers with a flowing skirt and a cinched-in waist. Against the red-gold of her hair, her skin glowed.

She was quite unprepared for his sudden question. 'Come with me to Farwell Cottage Hospital tonight,' he asked, 'to see Gwen?'

'But one of us will have to be here,' she frowned. 'What if you went this evening and I held the fort here, making my visit tomorrow?'

'Elissa,' he said very slowly, leaning forward with just a shadow of annoyance creeping over his face, 'I'm beginning to think there is something radically wrong with our relationship. Do you realise you jump out of your skin every time I come near you? And your avoidance of me is so obvious I'm beginning to feel as though I have a contagious disease.'

'That's silly,' she laughed lightly. 'We've just been busy this week!'

'Which is why I think we ought to make the effort to see Gwen this evening while we'll be relatively quiet.' He shrugged lightly. 'Harry will take any emergencies. As a matter of fact, I've already rung to arrange it.'

'Don't you think you should have consulted me first?' Elissa asked tightly.

'Well, it really doesn't matter whether you come or not,' he muttered grimly. 'I'll go by myself anyway. I'll give Gwen your regards.' He moved away from her, drawing off his white coat.

When he put it like that, Elissa realised she could hardly refuse to go with him. 'All right,' she called as he disappeared into the hall. 'I'll come with you. What time?'

He looked back round the door, slowly grinning. 'About seven.' Then hesitating, as his smile broadened, he asked, 'By the way, how has Barbara settled this week?'

Recollecting a little guiltily that she had deliberately avoided him over the last few days and very little news had passed between them, she nodded enthusiastically. 'Barbara's doing fine. She and Sharon work well together ... She's calm and patient with the clients and very keen on the pet healthcare classes. Actually, I don't know how she does it. With a family of three youngsters to look after, I'm sure I'd never cope.'

'I'm sure you would!' He ambled slowly back into the room and leaned a shoulder against the doorframe. 'Do you want children of your own, Elissa?'

The question was again so unexpected that she found herself blushing deeply. 'Well . . . Yes, of course. Doesn't every woman?'

'No, not every woman.' He sounded distant, almost as though he were talking to himself. 'For instance, Minty doesn't. Her career comes first. But then, she is very good at her job, first-class in fact.'

The mention of Minty brought all her emotions back into sharp focus and, though he had only said her name casually, Elissa was sure his thoughts were centred on the woman with whom he had once probably planned to have children before their engagement was broken.

Elissa tried to read his expression. Disappointment, frustration, hurt? She couldn't tell. As before, his face was shuttered.

★   ★   ★

Gwen Richards sat up in her bed, with huge dark eyes and gaunt cheeks. But the moment she saw them walk into her room, a smile brightened her face. Elissa had bought grapes from the kiosk on the ground floor, and Adam had bought flowers.

'I shall never be able to repay you for all you've done for me,' Gwen said after a while. 'You got Maddy seen to for me . . . and you rang the estate agents and told them I was here and now you're taking the trouble to visit with all these lovely gifts . . . '

Adam frowned at Elissa. Rather gruffly he asked, 'Have you thought about how you're going to recuperate, Gwen?'

She laid her grey head back on the pillow. 'I have to go back to the farm, I've no alternative until it sells.'

'Is there a relative or friend with whom you could stay?' Elissa asked, appalled at the thought of her having to endure such Spartan conditions.

Gwen remained silent. Elissa knew

she was too proud to say she couldn't afford a convalescence.

'Give this suggestion some thought,' Adam said very gently. 'I've a friend who has a convalescent home on the south coast, by the sea. He'd be happy to welcome you as a guest for a few months, or until the farm sold. Think it over and, if you like the idea, let me know and I'll make the necessary arrangements for you.'

'But I couldn't possibly!' Gwen sighed, near to tears.

When they left the ward, Elissa stopped outside the swing doors and looked anxiously back. Adam slid an arm round her shoulders. 'She'll be fine, don't worry. Gwen's a very proud woman — she's fended for herself so long it's difficult for her to accept help, but she'll come round, wait and see.'

'I hope so,' Elissa murmured doubt-fully. 'It was very thoughtful of you to make such a suggestion. She was obviously taken by surprise.'

He shrugged as they walked along

the corridor. 'I'm simply relieved she took it so well about Maddy.'

In the Mercedes, she clipped on her seatbelt and sat back. To her surprise, halfway home Adam said, 'A friend of mine lives this way. In our student days he specialised in orthopaedics and I went into ophthalmology. He and his wife are having a small get-together a week on Saturday — and before you say no, let me just add that Peter and Helen know quite a few people. The evening would be a good opportunity for us to promote Larkhill, especially on the referral side. It will probably mean talking a good deal of shop, but it will all be to a good purpose.'

She wondered apprehensively if this were another of Adam's joint-venture ideas. 'Will your guests be down again?' she asked cautiously.

He nodded. 'I think Minty and Philip have several more weekends scheduled in which to finish their work. I'm not sure what their plans are, but if they are staying — '

'You thought we could all go together?' Elissa supplied archly.

Jerking his head around at her tone, he said, 'Yes, why not?'

'I can't, I'm afraid.' Elissa shook her head firmly. 'I've other plans for that particular Saturday evening.'

Adam turned back to the road. 'Such as?'

Elissa said the first thing that came into mind. 'I'm going to see *A Midsummer Night's Dream*, a production put on by the medical students of Farwell Hospital in aid of charity.'

In fact, she had bought a ticket especially to give to Gwen, who was a keen fan of amateur dramatics. But now it would be put to another use.

'I had no idea you were interested in amateur dramatics,' he muttered, staring leadenly at the road. 'In fact I haven't ever heard you mention this fascinating hobby of yours before!'

Elissa was about to make a suitable retort when there was movement in the middle of the road just ahead of them.

'Look out, a rabbit!' she cried, putting her hand to her mouth.

Adam glanced in his mirror and flattened his foot on the brake, flicking off the engine. He jumped out, went round to the front, stooped down, and eventually returned with the rabbit in his hands cradled to his chest. 'I can't find any obvious damage,' Adam said as he slithered back into the driving seat. 'Looks in shock. Can you wrap him in the rug on the back seat and we'll pull in at the next lay-by.'

Elissa felt for the rug, laid it on her lap and transferred the rabbit into its warmth. 'His heartbeat is strong and his eyes are beginning to focus again,' she murmured as it began to struggle, and a couple of miles on Adam steered the car into a lay-by. His fingers came across to stroke behind the delicate grey ears.

'He'll be safer up there, by the tree.' Adam pointed.

The moon was a glowing silver, the night soft with scents and rippling breezes as Adam slipped an arm round her waist to help her up the steep embankment. At the top, by an English oak, under its spreading branches, they stood looking over the sleeping fields which ran away into the darkness and disappeared into a fine mist just beginning to roll over the heads of corn. A veil of stars and small puffy clouds shielded the black sky, changing its contours like a moving film above them.

'Let's release him just here,' Adam said, and he bent down to part the grass, revealing well-worn paths into the undergrowth where other creatures had scurried. Elissa bent down too and set the rabbit on the earth, unfolding the blanket. His tiny ears twitched and, with a kick of his back legs in the air, he scooted off.

She almost overbalanced as she stood up, one of her low-heeled pumps becoming stuck in a soft patch of earth. Adam reached out to catch her, and as he held her in his arms she could feel the strong beat of his heart against her own.

The moon was so bright that she could see herself reflected in the dark irises of his eyes, as her heart continued to pound like an express train.

'Why don't you give the ticket to Grace?' he said very softly. 'I know for certain Grace is a fan. She would be pleased with it. Then you'll be free to accept my invitation to Helen and Peter's.'

Hoping he couldn't see her revealing blush, Elissa tried to pull away. 'No, Adam!'

'But why?' He held her tighter. 'I mean, it just doesn't add up. You and I could be taking advantage of a perfect opportunity for PR!'

Losing patience, Elissa glared at him. 'Please let go of me, Adam. I can't come and there's an end to it.'

If the car had not caught them in its headlights and sounded its horn, Elissa realised that Adam might not have let her go. But on feeling him loosen his grip, she managed to side-step him and hurry to the Mercedes, her heart palpitating so fast that she felt sick and giddy. Flinging open the door and almost falling in, controlling the bout of trembling just before the driver's door swung open, she remained silent.

He slid in wordlessly and started the car, and for the rest of the way home Elissa did not make an attempt to speak, feeling the situation all the more soul-destroying when she realised, from the look on her companion's stony face, that he had even less wish to communicate now than she did.

*   *   *

The following day, Sunday, Elissa had a distress call from a farmer regarding his calving cow. She was relieved to have the excuse of leaving Larkhill and Adam's presence in the house.

As she drove in the Land Rover, her fingers gripped the wheel, showing white at the knuckles. A tightness in her chest heralded a huge, unexpected sob from deep inside, so that, shocking herself, she stopped the vehicle on the brow of a hill overlooking the sun-warmed countryside. She realised then, as she got out to take a deep breath, that it was not Adam whom she did not wish to come face to face with, but herself and her own emotions.

As she knew suddenly and clearly that what she had been fighting all this time was her growing love for him, her eyes smarted with unshed tears.

Living with Adam and his wife at Larkhill would surely be impossible! She found the landscape blurring before her, the rich yellows and browns merging into one pool of muddy colour as she imagined the future, understanding full well her dilemma.

With another painful sob in her throat she returned to the Land Rover and sat as the tears subsided, finally to be dried by the breeze which blew in from the open window. How foolish could she be? It was bad enough falling in love with a colleague with whom she had not yet forged professional roots, but it was even worse to fall in love with a man whose heart was already in the possession of another woman.

Some time later she drove into Greg Thornton's farm. Assessing the cow, she slipped on her delivery-gown and examined the area distended with calf.

'She's been straining for six hours,' Greg explained worriedly, 'and you can see he's there but I'm worried about giving her help 'case the cord is round his throat.'

Elissa nodded, sliding her hand down and feeling around the calf as the cow's contraction came.

'I can feel his mouth and bottom teeth, so the head is the right way up,' Elissa said with a little gasp of pain as, finding her arm trapped, she realised the calf was turning.

It was half an hour before Elissa managed to persuade the tiny unborn calf into a delivery position. She used all her strength, ignoring the discomfort of her own arms and the acute angle at which she had to work, but finally the calf was born and Greg assisted her as she laid it in the straw and the mother turned to stare at her offspring.

'I'd never give a little 'un like you credit for such strength,' Greg said ruefully, as they watched mother and calf together.

'Not altogether strength, Greg,' Elissa smiled, as she stripped off her protective clothing and washed her hands and arms in the warm water. 'Mostly patience, and a little luck.'

Elissa reflected, as she drove back to Larkhill, that she would need more than luck over the next few weeks for, now that she had admitted to herself the way she felt for Adam, how could she fail to recognise that her antipathy towards Minty was based purely on jealousy — the very same emotion which Adam felt towards Philip and which she had been all too ready to condemn?

9

The first hurdle over, of joining Adam at breakfast and trying to maintain a sensible conversation, mainly about Greg's cow and her calf, Elissa spent a few moments composing herself in her flat, wondering if it would be possible to share a future at Larkhill with the man she loved and the woman who would be his wife.

In the light of day, she knew it would not. There had to be an alternative. She couldn't think of one at the moment but, unless she wanted to endure the pain of unrequited love on a permanent basis, she must think of something.

'Two more patients for your weight-watching class,' Sharon explained as she met Elissa in the office. 'Bonnie and Clyde. A pair of gorgeous golden retrievers but really overweight. Mrs Preston sang your praises, apparently.

They live in the same street.'

Elissa met Bonnie and Clyde and duly invited them to the class tomorrow afternoon. In Reception she saw the shaggy Oscar, and recalled that Adam was seeing the Briard today.

He was soon greeting the female owner, who stared dismissively at Elissa as she swept past. Elissa wondered if her diagnosis of progressive retinal atrophy would prove correct and, if so, how the woman would deal with Adam's conclusions.

Later in the morning she found out, as she passed Adam in the passage. He stopped her briefly.

'You were absolutely right about the PRA on the Briard,' he said with a rueful smile. 'I can imagine the owner gave you a spot of trouble in accepting the diagnosis?'

Elissa nodded. 'Oscar was an expensive purchase, therefore he couldn't possibly have such a thing!'

'A misunderstanding I've corrected,' Adam said resolutely. 'Luckily this was central PRA which is characterised by the build-up of brown pigment in part of the retina and won't lead to complete blindness — although he will have problems with his middle field of vision throughout his life.' He shrugged. 'The fact Oscar is a Briard and cost a great deal doesn't alter the fact that either one of his parents, or even both, could have had the disease.'

'Can you help Oscar?' Elissa asked, as they walked along the hall.

Adam sighed. 'It's prevention rather than cure in PRA, as you know. The British Veterinary Association and Kennel Club and International Sheepdog Society have set up a scheme for the control of inherited diseases, whereby breeders submit their dogs voluntarily to examination by an eye panel. A pass certificate can be sent to the prospective buyer's vet by the panellists. As far as Oscar goes, his condition is non-painful, he'll probably adapt to his visual loss and, providing he's kept in his familiar surroundings on a lead when being exercised, he can still lead a happy life. But there's nothing I can do for him surgically.'

Feeling relieved that she had made the correct diagnosis, Elissa reflected that it was a great advantage to have Adam's speciality knowledge there, especially in a case like this. Then, with a despondent lurch of her heart, she recalled that whatever transformation for the better their professional rapport, and indeed the practice, had undergone, there could be no permanent future for them together at Larkhill.

'Oscar gave me an idea,' Adam said as they arrived in Reception. 'The veterinary nurse is ideally placed to give advice to our clients by heightening awareness of hereditary disorders such as PRA, even recommending the eye scheme before purchase. Perhaps Barbara could include this in one of the pet healthcare sessions you've been planning?'

Adam's enthusiasm was hard to match with any of her own. A shadow seemed cast over the day and she saw his puzzled glance as she nodded. All that she had striven for now seemed to be under threat: Larkhill, her father's practice, the house where she had grown up, everything that was dear to her.

'Cheer up,' Adam smiled at her. 'Whatever you're worrying about — it's not the end of the world, you know. Every problem has a solution.'

Back in her flat at lunchtime, Elissa made herself a cool drink and nibbled at a sandwich, thinking of what Adam had said. The solution to her problem, as far as she could see, was in taking one of two alternatives. Either she must move from the practice and allow Adam to buy her out — a heart-breaking decision — or the reverse. Would he consider an offer if she were to put one to him?

Finance was the first and most important factor. And here she had little choice. Failing a loan from the bank with high interest rates, she would have to sink her pride and discuss the matter with her godfather, who, after her father's death, had been prepared to help.

Shrugging away these depressing thoughts, Elissa decided to continue until she knew what was in Adam's mind.

The following morning, she assisted him with his second lens removal. This time, without instruction, she was able to monitor for him the machine which operated the microscope, adding the fluid to the cornea to lubricate it.

The dog, a small mongrel bitch, lay anaesthetised as Adam began to remove the milky-white substance, opening a circle in the lens capsule.

'Have you given any more thought to coming with me to Peter and Helen's?' he asked suddenly.

'Peter and Helen's?' Elissa repeated, startled.

'Yes, my friends who are having the small get-together, remember?' Elissa gazed at him in amazement. The bent dark head pressing the binocular of the microscope, the firm chin beneath, gave no indication that he was talking on a personal level.

She recovered with an effort, turning her attention back to the machine to operate the control which linked the microscope through ultra-sound. 'No,' she said a little unsteadily, 'I've given no more thought to it, because I've already told you I have other arrangements.'

'Which you refuse to postpone?'

Elissa changed the subject as a last line of defence. 'Shall I aspirate again?' she asked, her tone clearly cool.

There was a slight pause before a low, 'Yes.'

Watching him complete the opening of a full circle in the lens capsule, and with the jaws of miniature forceps removing the offending debris, Elissa felt her heart pound. But the delicate procedure continued in absolute silence with only the rhythmic bleeping of the ultra-sound machine.

Whatever had prompted him to bring the subject up must have been quickly forgotten as he completed the operation, his fingers working adeptly with the tiny diamond knife and miniature forceps.

At last, removing the four anchors on the eyelashes which had held them apart, and with a swift insertion of sutures to hold together the nipped eyelid, he nodded to her. 'Thanks. You've mastered the machine very well. It makes my task a lot easier.'

Elissa flushed. 'I'll fix the drip and help you with her into recovery.'

He glanced at her quickly, putting out a restraining hand. 'No, thanks, I can cope quite well now. You've your own surgery to attend to.'

For a moment she felt a pang of deep regret. She longed to turn to him and tell him how she felt. But that could never happen. How could she ever have allowed herself to fall into this situation, loving a man as much as she did, yet knowing there was no future, no hope at all for that love? And what happened to people, she wondered, when the suffering of unrequited love became too much, too distressful?

'I'll see you later, then,' Elissa said and, receiving no reply, she hurried out to disrobe in the prep-room. She was deep in thought as the water trickled over her hands and the soap smoothed in between her fingers — so deep that she only vaguely heard Sharon come in to deposit fresh towels in the dispenser.

'A kitten for vaccinations and a larger tom-cat with a bite,' Sharon said as she clipped the machine together and smiled, then stared at Elissa with a curious frown. 'Can you see them now?'

'Yes, yes, I'm coming,' Elissa said distractedly as Sharon left and cast a glance back to her.

'Oh . . . And by the way,' Sharon added hesitantly, 'there's been a call from someone for Adam. She wouldn't leave her name but said it was personal and she'd phone again. There was no message.'

Elissa nodded. Who else could it be but Minty?

She was particularly relieved when the

afternoon arrived and Barbara directed the deluge of dogs into Reception for roll-call.

Mrs Preston stood with Lavender on the doorstep, looking for Elissa. When she found her, surrounded by the golden retrievers and their owners, she burst out, 'I've lost three pounds! Can you see it? Look — here!' She pinched a handful of skirt at her waist.

At this piece of excited news there was a stir in the room and it was several moments before Barbara managed to restore silence.

'Very impressive!' Elissa encouraged and, though taken by surprise, she could see that her client certainly looked much brighter if not altogether thinner. 'How about Lavender?'

'We've eaten no midnight snacks,' Mrs Preston announced proudly. 'You're right, she enjoyed the walk around the garden more. And so did I, I think!'

Everyone laughed and Elissa breathed a sigh of relief that at least one of her worries had not materialised in the form of a defeated Mrs Preston. When Lavender was weighed, however, she remained the same weight. 'We'll reduce her allowance by twenty per cent,' Elissa decided as she stroked a far-too-satisfied Lavender, who looked as though she were getting just a little more at supper-time than she ought.

'Maybe I have been a bit heavy-handed,' Mrs Preston admitted, blushing. 'But at least she hasn't put any on and that's what she's been doing for weeks!'

Giving both the benefit of the doubt, Elissa handed Mrs Preston the weight-graph with a rueful, 'The scales never lie, don't forget!'

In the garden, Adam had set the chairs as before. When everyone had taken their seats, the results of the weighing were discussed and Barbara, who had already prepared a profile of obesity in dogs, asked the gathering for their observations on overweight.

'Bonnie and Clyde bolt their food and then ask for more,' the newcomer complained.

'Never give them it,' Barbara advised firmly. 'Offer water afterwards and a change of scenery, but never any more food.'

'Badger begs for food at mealtimes, we just can't stop him,' another client sighed.

'Then occupy him in another room, with a toy or ball, or just switch on the radio. Dogs like to be kept company and he won't hear the noise the family is making then and feel deprived. Put temptation out of his reach and out of yours too.'

'Wilbur sleeps instead of playing and refuses to walk more than short distances,' said a woman with a very fat beagle who had fallen asleep. He batted a lazy eyelid at the mention of his name. 'I think he's miserable because he's so hungry.'

Barbara asked the owner for his lead, gave it a brisk tug and Wilbur, though reluctant, stretched his short legs. After several laps of the garden, Barbara came back with a big smile and a panting but perky Wilbur. 'He's as bright as a button once you get him going. Don't let him have his own way, especially at the beginning of his new diet and exercise regime. Once he starts to lose weight, you won't be able to stop him. Elissa has put Wilbur on canned food with a high moisture content so that hunger-misery is reduced to a minimum. Really, he's quite satisfied — and he's lost a kilogram too.' She paused, glancing at Mrs Preston. 'We can see the improvement with Mrs Preston. What a difference just a few pounds make!'

Elissa found herself grinning as Mrs Preston almost took a bow. Barbara had captured everyone's interest and, because of that, together with Mrs Preston's personal success, Elissa handed out tea feeling particularly cheerful.

Until she saw Adam coming across the lawn followed by Arnie. He mingled with the group, finally managing to tear himself away and come over to her. 'I've just had a call from Mr Martin. The ward sister allowed him to use the mobile telephone.'

'How is he feeling?' Elissa asked, concerned.

'Very well, considering the gravity of the operation. But he's been worrying about Arnie.'

'You mean, how he will cope with him during his convalescence.'

Adam nodded. 'His recently widowed brother in Wales has asked him if he would like to share a house with him. It would mean a new start and certainly less rent and overheads. But the brother has an allergy to dogs' hair, so it would be impossible for him to take Arnie.'

Elissa sighed. 'What a difficult decision.'

Adam ran a hand through his hair, frowning. 'On the spur of the moment I offered to have Arnie permanently, since he's settled so well with us.' Apologetically he glanced at her. 'Then I realised I should have discussed matters with you first.'

Under normal circumstances, Elissa reflected, she would not have hesitated in agreeing to offer Arnie a home, but her future was uncertain and to take on the responsibility of a dog at Larkhill at this stage was unfair. Adam had had no such qualms of course, since as far as he was concerned Larkhill offered all the permanency he had planned for both Arnie and himself — and Minty.

'Yes, you should have discussed the matter with me first, Adam. Surely you stopped to think . . . ' She shook her head in frustration. 'Oh, well, it doesn't matter now, I suppose.'

The dark eyes narrowed. 'I didn't imagine you would take it like this! I thought you would be only too pleased to give Arnie a home.' He stooped to stroke Arnie, who lifted his head, and her heart gave a little twist. 'Oh, well, if that's the way you feel, I'd better phone the old chap back and tell him.'

He went to move, but she put out a hand. 'Perhaps . . . Well, maybe you felt you had no other alternative but to offer.' She felt inexcusably churlish and, hating herself for the way she sounded, she realised how her imprisoned feelings for Adam would gradually inhibit their working relationship too. 'Of course Arnie is welcome at Larkhill,' she sighed with a small shrug, knowing it was useless trying to hide the truth from herself, even if she could from Adam.

Concluding the afternoon, Elissa saw to the last of the group and bade Barbara farewell at five. The day had been an outstanding success, but Elissa felt so disheartened by the thoughts which kept slipping into her mind that she missed supper completely. Trying unsuccessfully to distract her thoughts and lose herself in a novel, she reflected that one way or another she would have to solve her problem soon or Adam would discover the truth of her true feelings. And surely there would be no worse humiliation than that?

★ ★ ★

The problem came to a head sooner than Elissa had imagined, for on Thursday, as she walked from her flat early in the morning, Adam was standing in the hall, talking on the telephone. She knew by the look on his face who the caller was.

Replacing the receiver, he called to her. 'That was Minty. She and Philip are travelling from London today, earlier than planned.'

Elissa felt her heart skip a beat. 'I've told you before, Adam, it makes no difference to me when your guests arrive.' Once again, despising herself for lying, she turned quickly and hurried along to the kitchen where she struck up a conversation with Grace, trying to take her mind off the mixture of anguish and panic which churned inside her.

Elissa tried to be objective and to concentrate on her work. But her worst expectations were realised at half-past five, when the sound of the Porsche caused her to glance through the reception window. Philip was tugging out cases and Minty was walking with Adam into the house.

Entering Larkhill by the connecting door, Elissa had no illusions as to what she might discover this time.

'Elissa!' Minty cried as she disentangled herself from Adam. She was wearing a frothy blue dress, with dark hair exotically plaited from the crown of her head. 'How nice to see you again. I hope we haven't put you to any trouble?'

'Hello, Minty.' Elissa smiled. Whatever happened from now on, it was obvious that Minty had won him back and she must privately endure the fact until she found some solution for herself. 'No, no trouble at all,' she replied sweetly.

It did not mean, however, she told herself as she avoided Adam's gaze, that this awful charade had to be prolonged indefinitely. Even as she stood there, a decision had already sprung to mind at the moment of witnessing Minty in his arms. At the first opportunity she would call and see her godfather and discuss the matter of a loan, which she would then offer to Adam in the hope that he would consider it.

In the morning she rang her god-father and asked if she could see him as soon as possible. Making a time for Saturday afternoon at his practice, she was relieved that he would see her there rather than at his home where there might be interruptions.

The rest of the morning seemed a blur to Elissa as she tried to concentrate on the few clients who came in with assorted complaints: a cat with an abscess for draining, several vaccinations, and a lame dog who had torn his front leg on barbed wire and needed several sutures.

At lunchtime, Philip, whom she had met briefly as she left the house this morning, came into the practice. Surprised, Elissa looked up from the office desk where she was working. 'Come for a drink and a sandwich,' he invited her cheerfully. 'It's such a beautiful day.'

She smiled vaguely. 'Some other

time, Philip. I'm afraid we've a busy afternoon. I've a surgery in three quarters of an hour.' She paused. 'Aren't you and Minty working today?'

Philip shrugged. 'Minty's sunbathing in the garden at the moment.'

Elissa nodded. 'And you're bored, I suppose?'

He laughed. 'I wouldn't be if you'd come out with me. What about this evening, after work? You and I will both be redundant. Adam's taking Minty to dinner.'

Elissa took a small breath. No doubt a proposal was in Adam's mind.

'Is that a yes?' Philip looked expectant. What, Elissa wondered dismally, would be the harm in spending one evening in his company? Perhaps it might even do them both some good.

'If I can get Harry's surgery to cover for a couple of hours,' she agreed hesitantly.

To her surprise he bent down and kissed her briefly. As he drew away, she saw that behind him stood Adam.

Philip looked back to her with a wink. 'See you this evening.'

When he had gone, Adam said, 'So I was right. You are involved with Philip Saville?'

Elissa's face turned scarlet. 'Don't be ridiculous, Adam! What a stupid thing to say.'

'Then I haven't disturbed a romantic moment?' he asked sarcastically. 'I rather thought I had.'

'Because you've drawn all the wrong conclusions,' Elissa returned sharply as his insinuation stung. But it also made her angry. 'Philip was just being friendly . . . ' Shaken, she wondered why she was defending herself and added crisply, 'Frankly, it's none of your business anyway, Adam.'

He thrust the papers he was holding down on the desk. 'No, it isn't, you're quite right. It's up to you whether or not you choose to become involved with a dubious individual like Philip Saville.'

Elissa gasped at his open hostility. 'What on earth do you mean by that?'

He shrugged dismissively. 'If you can't see the man for what he is underneath all that charm, then nothing I can say will influence you.'

Elissa caught her breath. 'And what does Minty think of your opinion of Philip?'

He paused, frowning. 'Minty? Why should I discuss Philip with her? He's her professional colleague. They're not entangled in a romantic relationship. It's you I'm concerned about.' Then, as his dark brows drew together over glittering eyes, he laughed derisively. 'But I seem to be wasting my breath with useless warnings!' He turned and walked to the door, stopping himself just before closing it. 'The reason I stopped by was because I've just had a call from Helen. She's trying to get some idea of numbers for their party on Saturday night.' He smiled sardonically. 'Perhaps the fact Philip is joining us will offer a certain appeal to the evening and cause you to change your mind about coming?'

Exasperated, she glared at him. 'Yes, you're right, it does!' She just managed to stop herself from adding that having Philip occupied for the evening would no doubt suit his own purposes very well too. 'I find Philip stimulating company, as it happens,' she added tartly.

There was a tense moment when she thought he was going to reply to her challenge, but then he merely took a breath and noded abruptly, before leaving the room without a word more.

Elissa knew it was a mistake to go with Philip for a drink, much more to have agreed in a moment of anger to the party invitation. She was doing both now, to spite Adam, which of course was the worst reason possible.

Hoping her godfather's surgery would be too busy to step in and take calls that evening, she was bitterly disappointed when they said they could.

She worried the rest of the day, Adam's insinuations only making her more disturbed as she went over them in her mind, disclosing his deep and unfounded dislike of the other man. Even so, as the day wore on, she wished she had never agreed to go out with Philip. There was nothing between them, certainly not on her side. The kiss had surprised her very much, and she regretted bitterly that Adam should have witnessed it, precipitating the resulting argument.

Philip took her to a country pub. She drank white wine and tried to avoid all reference to Minty and Adam. But Philip seemed intent on drawing the conversation round to them.

'Adam looked pretty unhappy about us this morning,' he said, sipping his drink. 'Are you sure you two haven't something between you?'

Elissa shook her head, annoyed at his presumption. 'We're just partners, as I've already told you. I think kissing me the way you did would have made anyone walking in on us look embarrassed!'

'Only a little harmless fun,' he grinned, slipping his arm round her. 'It was just bad luck Adam happened to walk in at the wrong time. But then, if you're not having an affair with him, what is there to worry about?'

'I'm not worried. But I simply don't want Adam or you, Philip, to misunderstand — '

'There's no harm in what we did, Elissa. You're taking things far too seriously. You're a beautiful young woman. I just made the mistake of kissing you in your place of work and not in some more romantic setting.'

Elissa stiffened. 'Philip . . . perhaps I should make it clear. I like you. I enjoy your company, but — '

'Then it's a start,' he cut in with a grin. 'I asked you to come out with me just to get to know you a little better. OK, there's no big chemical reaction between us but perhaps there could be if you gave us a chance. If you want my opinion, you work too hard. At your age you should be letting your hair down and having some fun.'

Elissa realised then that she had

made a wrong decision in coming tonight. She and Philip had little in common, and Adam's words vaguely passed through her mind. 'Let's go for a walk and get some fresh air, shall we?' she suggested brightly. 'It's such a lovely evening and I have to be back before long.'

'You really are a little Cinderella!' he laughed. 'But, yes, let's go for a romantic stroll!'

She regretted her request instantly. The luxurious car sped them along the country lanes, but Philip's conversation of the city and of his work in commercial design left her cold. She thought of Adam and Minty enjoying the evening together, and wished she were at least at home with Arnie.

Philip parked the car on a hill which overlooked the River Severn, coiling like a silver snake through the green fields below. If she had been here with someone she loved, it would have been the perfect place to spend an hour at the close of day. They walked a little, but Elissa glanced at her watch, sensing it was best to return as darkness fell.

'Cinderella,' taunted Philip again, as the breeze lifted her golden-brown hair from her slender neck, and she shivered. 'Always having to return by midnight in case the surgery turns into a pumpkin!'

Elissa laughed half-heartedly, but turned back all the same. 'By the time we get home it will be rather late,' she said firmly.

'Oh, come on!' Philip took her hand to stop her. 'You'll make me think there's something wrong with me!'

Elissa slipped out of his grasp and began to walk quickly on. He caught up with her, his face angry. 'Why not make the most of the evening,' he demanded as they walked, 'instead of rushing back? Adam's occupied with Minty. He probably won't even know you've come out with me.'

Elissa stopped, her cheeks inflamed at the suggestion. 'So you think I'm here behind Adam's back — you really think he and I are ... are having an affair?'

'Yes. Why not? There's something going on between you. He didn't give me that warning look for nothing when he caught us kissing today. And the way he watches you, that look in his eyes . . . Oh, sure, he's involved with Minty too, but perhaps he's the kind of man who likes a touch of variety in his life.'

She was too upset to speak. Instead, she hurried as fast as she could to the car. He caught up with her, clutching her arm. Her heart banged in fright as he laughed scornfully. 'You're just a little tease, Elissa!'

She pulled her arm away. 'I owe you no explanation, Philip. Now, please, I'd like to go home!'

She almost ran the last few yards to the Porsche and was relieved as she tugged at the door to find it open.

Philip drove in angry silence and too fast. Elissa held on to the seat, regretting that she had had the naïveté to think he wanted her friendship when all along he'd suspected her of having an affair with Adam and the capability

271

of indulging in a fling with him too.

When they arrived back at Larkhill it was dark and the car slid to a halt.

'Just a kiss goodnight,' Philip whispered tensely and, preventing her from climbing out, he stretched his arm across. 'It can't do any harm and we probably won't have much of a chance to see one another again. Your boyfriend will never know.'

Suddenly she realised just how right Adam had been in his warnings. Philip was obviously a man without scruple and wouldn't bat an eyelid when it came to making a pass.

She sat trapped, her heart pounding. 'Please don't let's spoil this evening, Philip. I don't want to quarrel with you, but you've completey the wrong idea of — '

His mouth came down on hers, insistent and hard, silencing her, his hands going over her bare arms, bringing her roughly towards him.

She struggled bitterly, but he was far too strong. Realising that he had no intention of releasing her, she fumbled in panic for the door-handle.

He guessed her intention and grabbed back her hand, his other locking round her waist, jerking her towards him so that the breath left her body in a rush. 'What's the big deal, Elissa? You knew when you agreed to come out with me that the evening would end like this.'

'Stop it, Philip!' she cried, lashing out as he tried to kiss her again. Her wail seemed to echo around the car.

As she cried out, a face appeared at the window. She didn't know how long Adam had been standing there, but he hammered a fist on the glass.

Philip let her go, cursing under his breath. He hardly had time to open his door before it was jerked fully open by Adam.

'What's going on?' Adam demanded, looking in at Elissa.

'Nothing that concerns you!' Philip pushed himself up in fury from the seat.

Elissa climbed out too, her legs like water.

'Are you all right?' Adam asked her over the roof of the Porsche.

'Of course she is!' Philip interrupted with a grimace.

'You'd better go indoors,' Adam muttered as he looked into her pale face.

As Elissa passed, Minty climbed out of the Mercedes parked by the house, but neither of them spoke. Hurrying in, Elissa heard raised voices in the distance.

Minutes later she was in her own flat and, despite trembling like a leaf, she took a deep breath, realising that there was nothing for it but to accept the events of the disastrous evening and try to put them behind her.

Suddenly, however, there was a knock at the door and her heart took a downward dive as she wondered if it was Philip in an even angrier mood. But when she opened the door, Adam stood there, his face thunderous.

'Do you want to come in?' she asked, managing to keep her voice level.

'No, thank you.' His dark eyes were glinting angrily. 'But I would like to know just what you think you're playing at?'

Elissa frowned. 'What on earth do you mean?'

'Why didn't you admit to your affair with Philip?' he demanded. 'I just made a damn fool of myself out there thinking you were in trouble.'

Elissa caught her breath. 'We aren't having an affair! We simply went for a walk this evening — '

'Philip's explained, so you needn't bother!' Adam muttered darkly, giving her no time to say more. 'I'm an absolute fool. I should have known when I saw him kissing you this morning.'

'But you don't understand, you don't want to understand!' Elissa shook her head helplessly. Nothing she said now would make any difference. Whatever Philip had told him certainly suited him better than the real truth, which he obviously didn't want to hear from her lips.

He turned and left her without uttering another word, and Elissa fell against the closed door, her eyes brimming over with tears.

10

Elissa bent to check the little mongrel who had made such a good recovery after her eye operation. She was quite happy as she barked in delight, scampering around the garden kennel which she had occupied for the last twenty-four hours. Adam's patient was fully recovered, due to be discharged this morning. That would mean he would be coming in to see his client, Elissa reflected, as she walked the dog on the lead.

After last night, she would have preferred to avoid everyone, but there seemed no hope of that as, returning the dog to the kennel and going back into Reception, she glanced out of the window to see Minty walking to the Porsche with a camera slung across her shoulder. Not that Minty would be coming into the surgery. She was obviously going with Philip to the manor house.

Suddenly the door opened and her first Saturday morning patient, a tiny hedgehog, was brought in by a young woman. 'I thought he was lame,' she explained, as she followed Elissa along to her consulting-room. 'But I think perhaps he was born with a bad foot.'

Elissa studied the little ball of prickles. It unrolled in the box and a tiny snout came up to sniff around. One foot was a peculiar shape, but even so he managed to patrol his box quite well.

'I've fed him through a syringe on goat's milk,' the young girl explained, 'and he's thriving. But I can't seem to get rid of those things in between his spines.'

Elissa looked more closely. 'Yes, they're ticks, actually. I'll give him an injection of Ivomec which will effectively remove all parasites. You've done very well to keep him alive.'

Elissa gave the injection and then carefully placed the hedgehog on her scales. 'He's not quite up to one point two-five pounds and you won't be able to release him safely until he's reached this safe weight. I'll give you a preparation called Panacur which will deal with any worms. Just mix it with his food.'

The girl nodded. 'He's eating tinned cat-food quite happily now.'

They watched the hedgehog curl up in his box and Elissa walked back into Reception with them, suddenly aware of more movement outside the window. She saw Minty again in her white leggings and a crimson blouse, her hair falling loose around her shoulders, leaning against the Porsche, this time deep in conversation with Adam.

Elissa forced away her gaze. 'Thank you for bringing him in,' she said distractedly to the girl, opening the door.

'I must pay you.' The girl moved the box to hold on her hip, and unclipped her purse.

Elissa shook her head. 'No, the treatment is free of charge. Wild animals are an exception and we like to encourage people to do as you have done and care for them. But thank you anyway.'

When the girl had gone, Elissa walked back to her consulting-room without looking through the window. Sharon was having this morning off, and the surgery was unusually quiet without the activity behind the reception desk. With no patients in the waiting-room, Elissa walked slowly down the passageway.

She realised that her feelings were becoming out of hand. The pain she felt was jealousy as her heart ached and her stomach knotted into a fist. What right did she have to be jealous? None at all. Minty had warned her from the very start that she had set her cap at winning Adam back, Now it was evident that she had. The sooner the situation could be dealt with as a whole the better. If she had had any uncertainties about seeing her godfather this afternoon, they were now all gone.

A few minutes later, Elissa heard a

noise as she was tidying the instruments in her consulting-room. She turned to discover Philip watching her and she took a startled step backwards.

'Don't be alarmed,' he said, as he hovered in the doorway. 'I've come to apologise, Elissa. I'm afraid I frightened you and spoiled things for everyone last night simply because I couldn't get my own way.' He made no move to come in, and she realised that he did actually mean what he said as he added softly, 'Is there something I can do to make amends?'

All her anger seemed to evaporate as she saw how miserable he was. OK, he'd made a clumsy pass and wouldn't take no for an answer and scared her too, but it wasn't a hanging offence. As far as the story he'd told Adam was concerned, well, she supposed he'd done it out of spite, and she could understand that particular emotion too.

'There isn't anything you can do, Philip,' she said with a shrug. 'I would have liked us to be friends, but it seems that wasn't what you had in mind.'

He looked repentant, his blue eyes shadowed. 'Quite honestly, I'm not used to your sort of girl. I've found women don't usually mean what they say,' he admitted, looking at her under his fair lashes. 'It's a kind of game I'm used to playing and I suppose . . . '

'And you thought I was playing too?'

He didn't reply, but she understood his silence.

'Perhaps in future you won't make that assumption with all women,' Elissa said with a wry smile.

Thoughtfully, he nodded. 'Perhaps I won't.'

She shrugged lightly. 'You probably aren't aware, but the practice means a great deal to me, Philip, more since Dad died. I've thought about very little other than getting it back on its feet.'

'Does that include men?' he asked cryptically.

Up until the time she had met Adam Kennedy, she could have said this was true, but now, falling in love seemed to be her sole preoccupation, and she blushed guiltily as Philip stared at her curiously.

'You're in love with Adam, aren't you, and he doesn't know?' he murmured, watching her, then, as she went to protest, he held up his hand. 'No, don't answer that one. Apart from it suddenly dawning on me that was the way you felt about him, I realised just what a mess I've made of everything. And there's more too ... I have a confession to make ... and I'm not sure if you'll ever be able to forgive me for this.'

Elissa flushed involuntarily and said sharply, 'You mean the tale you told Adam about us, I suppose?'

'You know?' Philip asked with a start. His face went red. 'Elissa, I'm really sorry. I don't know why I let Adam think he was butting his nose into an affair we had going between us. It was unforgivable of me ... '

'Yes, it was,' Elissa agreed bitterly, going cold at the thought of the scene between her and Adam last night. But what was done, was done. If Adam wanted to believe Philip's imaginative stories rather than give her a chance to explain, then let him. 'It really doesn't matter now,' she sighed as he looked crestfallen. 'Let's just put the evening behind us, Philip.'

'I'll speak to Adam later today when Minty and I return, and I'll explain everything to him then,' Philip said hurriedly.

Elissa shook her head. 'No, I'd prefer it if you'd just leave the whole thing alone now. It's best forgotten.'

He frowned. 'If you're sure — '

Before he could complete his sentence, Adam walked in. This time, Elissa noticed that it was Philip who looked uncomfortable. He said swiftly, 'I must be on my way. We have to get quite a lot of work done this weekend.'

When he had gone, Adam merely glanced at his watch. 'My client should be here soon,' he said crisply, not bothering with salutations, 'to collect her little mongrel.'

His icy tone cut her to the quick. 'I've walked her this morning. She's very perky,' Elissa said, with an effort at normality.

He nodded. 'She's made an excellent recovery, just as Breeze did. Doesn't like the gauze on her eye very much, so I'm removing that this morning. In less than a week, though, she'll have full sight restored.'

He talked as though nothing at all had happened last night. It was obvious that this was the way he was going to address the situation and, as far as Elissa was concerned, she would have to accept it.

But it was with another aching pang of regret that she knew she would not be able to share again in such triumphs as Breeze and this little mongrel. Her fine eyebrows pleated in the middle as she could not hide from herself a fresh surge of hopeless disappointment as she thought of the future.

* * *

'The answer, Elissa,' said Harry Fitzroy, 'is yes. Of course I'll help. Louise and I wanted to in the first place. But we knew how independent you were. Quite frankly, we admired your choice in Adam. May I ask what's changed your mind?'

Elissa sat stiffly in a chair in her godfather's office. 'Personal differences. Ones we can't resolve,' she admitted evasively.

'They must be very severe,' her godfather observed as he watched her.

'I shouldn't be asking for your help if they weren't,' Elissa sighed dismally. 'I simply feel I must ask Adam if he would consider me buying him out before . . . before either of us begins to plan for the future.'

Her godfather frowned. 'I'm surprised at this turn of events, really I am. I thought the pair of you were getting on so well.'

She could hardly look her godfather

in the eye. 'I think we could resolve superficial professional differences,' she said, carefully choosing her words, 'but personally we don't seem to be . . . compatible.' Should she tell Harry the whole truth, she wondered? This was far more difficult than she had imagined it was going to be. She added reluctantly, 'You see, the problem is I'm afraid I don't have much of a rapport with his fiancée, or at least his ex-fiancée. We don't see eye to eye at all and I know if she and Adam . . . were to marry . . . Oh, Harry, do you under-stand what I'm saying?'

He rested back in his chair with a sigh. 'Oh, dear, Elissa. I didn't realise there was a third party.'

Elissa felt that she sounded like a woman spurned. Whatever would her godfather think? Trying to recover a little lost pride, she added in a rush, 'Adam was engaged before he left for the States, but because of the separa-tion, I understand the engagement was broken off. She . . . That is . . . Minty

Gale told me she intended to win Adam back and I think the only reason she accepted work in this area was for that express purpose. Unfortunately . . . I allowed myself to . . . to — '

'Fall in love,' Harry supplied for her.

Elissa nodded. 'I feel such a fool.'

The old vet regarded her with deep concern. 'Falling in love is not so foolish, my dear. I'd rather hoped . . . Well, being the old busybody I am, I tried several times to winkle information out of Adam regarding you two. He wouldn't say a word, but I gathered the impression he was very fond of you. I had no idea there was another woman involved.'

'Not just another woman,' Elissa reminded him, smiling bravely. 'A fiancée.'

'Such a pity. You two would have made good practice partners, and with a practice like Larkhill . . . ' He shrugged heavily. 'Of course the offer of financial help is still open to you. But even so, perhaps you had better discuss this with Adam before we go any further. He may well wish to remain at Larkhill, since he's firmly established his unit there.'

Elissa had given much thought to this. He had indeed entrenched himself deeply into her life, almost without her knowing. At first, she had resisted every effort on his part, unwilling to accept his presence at Larkhill after her father's death. But the inner battle of her emotions hadn't left her in peace. All through the refurbishment she had wrestled with her own confused feelings, suppressing her resentment at what were perfectly justified suggestions on his part. When he'd kissed her she'd known there was a strong physical attraction, but even then, she had ignored the burning desire of her own heart. And then suddenly, as though a veil had been drawn from her eyes, she understood what it was like to see properly, to fall in love, to want someone so much . . .

'Elissa?' Her godfather's concerned voice broke into her thoughts.

She nodded, smiling weakly. 'Yes, I've taken that into consideration, Harry. If Adam doesn't want to leave Larkhill, then there's only one other alternative. I shall have to move away.'

Harry looked shocked. 'But Larkhill is your home!'

Resolutely Elissa met his shocked gaze, her green eyes moist. 'I shall have to find another one. Begin again. Make a fresh start with a new practice somewhere.'

'I would advise you to think hard, Elissa. Talk to Adam and discuss the problem seriously. Perhaps you could work out a compromise.'

Elissa knew there was none. The way she felt about Adam left her with only two alternatives. Standing up before her godfather should see she was on the brink of tears, she said unsteadily, 'I've made up my mind, Harry. All I can do is ask Adam if he will consider my offer.'

* * *

The next day, Sunday, Elissa decided to visit Gwen. Since it was Adam's turn to be on call, she left just after lunch, buying flowers in the village and arriving at the hospital in time to meet Gwen using her walking-frame for the first time, with the aid of a nurse.

Elissa took over, guiding Gwen to a chair in the sunny lounge. The wing of the hospital was new. Some of the patients sat out in the flowered garden, but Gwen was content to sit on the brand-new easy chair and look out of the window.

'Have you thought any more about Adam's offer?' Elissa asked, when the tea was brought round and Gwen seemed relaxed enough to talk about the future.

She nodded. 'It was very kind of him. I think I'd like to have a change of scenery, but I'm worried about paying. What if the farm doesn't sell?'

Elissa laughed lightly. 'Of course it will! There's no problem with the finances. Eventually it will go, but until it does, Adam explained you have no financial worry.'

At last Gwen nodded. 'Will you thank your young man for me?'

Elissa blushed deeply. 'He's not . . . We aren't a couple, Gwen, just practice partners.'

A small smile touched the older woman's lips. 'Then you'll have to tell him that too, won't you, Elissa?' she laughed. 'If there's one thing I am still able to recognise, it's love in someone's eyes. And that young man has eyes for no one else but you.'

Elissa managed to change the direction of the conversation after that, her heart aching with the knowledge that Gwen had seen love in Adam's eyes, but it was love for Minty, not her. To explain the whole thing would be just too painful, and besides, Gwen was probably still very vague after her illness.

She hugged her goodbye at teatime, noticing that Gwen's eyes were almost closing in the warmth of the room.

Walking along the corridor, she remembered the last time she had walked this way with Adam. Was it then that she had begun to accept she was falling in love with him?

Driving past the wildlife park on the way home, she decided against calling in to enquire after Trinka and Honeybunch. The trouble was that just about everything in her life reminded her of Adam, and yet . . .

How long had she known him? A matter of weeks? And yet, she wondered as she drove up to Larkhill and saw the familiar bower of honeysuckle enveloping the door, would she ever learn to live without him?

★   ★   ★

Minty and Philip she did not see again that weekend. She guessed they were gone for, by the time she returned from the hospital, the Porsche was absent from its parking place and had not returned by nightfall.

Elissa heard Adam calling to Arnie in the garden at dusk, and she watched through her window, running her eyes over the tall dark shape, hungry, in spite of herself, for the sight and sound of his presence.

She left going to bed until late, wondering if he might call, torn between her desire to see him and her inner voice of common sense which told her that the last thing he had on his mind was to talk to her.

Monday crawled in slowly through her window, a grey, overcast early morning, and her green eyes were dulled by a fitful night of tossing and turning.

The week began its now familiar pattern, with a full waiting-room, the clients equally divided between her and Adam. She told Adam of her visit to Gwen and he seemed pleased that she had taken up the offer of convalescence. But they had little chance to talk again until the end of the day, when, with both their lists completed, he strolled into her consulting-room with Arnie padding beside him. He handed her a letter. 'It's from Mr Martin, thanking us,' he explained.

Elissa read it, moved by the old man's grateful words. She folded it up and returned it to the envelope, looking up at Adam. 'I can understand him not being able to see Arnie before he leaves for Wales. I don't think I could if I was in his position.'

As if Arnie understood, he ambled towards her and rubbed his bristly chin on her hand. She bent down and slid her arm around his neck. 'But you'll be happy here,' she whispered. 'You'll love Larkhill, even if . . . '

Her eyes were suddenly moist and she laid her cheek against Arnie's fur. Soon she must tell Adam what was in her mind.

'I thought I'd give Arnie a walk along the bridle-path,' Adam said suddenly. 'Sharon can take any messages. Do you feel like some fresh air?'

Elissa nodded. 'Yes, good idea,' she

agreed brightly, blinking back her unhappiness as she took off her white coat.

She was wearing a cool ivory silk blouse and a thin navy-blue pencil skirt which, in the heat, moulded gently to her slender curves. Self-consciously she drew back her thick hair, aware of Adam's gaze. Perhaps it was the heat, but the tiny hairs on the back of her neck seemed to stand on end and she shivered, avoiding his eyes and the long, intense stare.

Summer smelt like burnt cinnamon as they walked from Larkhill to the woods across the road. The bracken trail was dry and crackled under their feet and the sun warmed their faces through the silver trees.

As they walked, she wondered why she couldn't have fallen in love while she was at college, or fallen in love in Africa, and then at least she could have left love behind. But the irony was that she had travelled thousands of miles to come back full circle to heartache, to this place of her childhood.

'A penny for your thoughts?' he asked in a low voice.

'Do you really want to know?'

'I wouldn't ask otherwise. You've had something on your mind for quite a while, haven't you?' He stopped, staring down at her with a concerned frown.

Suddenly she seemed to lose courage. Then, knowing this was the point of no return, she gathered all her resources. 'Adam, our partnership just isn't working out. Perhaps it's a personality clash — perhaps we just can't get along as we thought we would — but — '

'I'm sorry, I don't understand,' he broke in sharply. 'I'm aware we've had our differences and I was to blame this weekend for losing my temper, but I can't see that's reason enough for us to fall out.'

'It's not as simple as reducing it to one weekend,' Elissa protested, walking on, avoiding his gaze. 'I honestly don't feel we are compatible as partners.'

He laid a hand on her arm to stop her. 'You don't think?' he demanded angrily. 'What about me? Doesn't my view count?'

She took a breath. 'Yes, of course it does! That's why I'm trying to discuss this with you rationally.'

'Hardly rational — the idea we can't solve our problems, whatever they are, together, as practice partners!' He shook his head. 'I don't believe this. There's something more, isn't there?'

Petrified that he might force her into an admission, Elissa began to panic. 'I want . . . That is, I would like to offer to buy you out,' she stammered, as her cheeks flushed crimson. 'I know you've put a great deal of energy into Larkhill . . . I want to compensate you for the refurbishment of the surgery — the equipment, the time and the effort — '

'As easily as that?' Anger tightened the muscles of his face as he cut her short. 'You just want to give up everything we've worked for because we've had a few misunderstandings, is that it?'

'Don't make this any harder for me, please,' she begged as he stared at her incredulously. 'Separating will be in our best interests, Adam, though you may not see why at the moment.'

'Too damn right I don't see why!' he exploded. 'What if I refuse? What then?'

'Adam . . . You can't . . . Oh, please be reasonable . . . ' Suddenly she burst into tears, her voice choked into a whisper as she put her fingers up to hide her face.

Strong brown hands came up to remove them as he brushed the wild waves from her wet face. 'Oh, Elissa . . . what's happening?' he muttered as he brought her gently into his arms, the anger on his face fading. 'Why do you want to leave me?' he whispered, moving up her chin with his thumbs so that he could stare into her eyes as though looking for an answer.

'It . . . it's for the best,' she stammered, knowing he was going to kiss her, knowing she was going to be unable to move away, to do anything about the waves of love flowing through her. Sad, despairing love which she could not express and which was doomed forever after this moment.

Knowing she had lost the battle to refuse herself this one last kiss, opening her mouth to his warmth as he brought her firmly towards him, she yielded, her breasts throbbing as he pressed her against his chest, pounding heart against pounding heart, his lips moving searchingly over hers, his tongue entering between her small white teeth.

A shiver of arousal went through her as she tasted the indescribable sweetness of his mouth, losing herself in paradise for a few brief moments, knowing deep inside herself that this was much more than an ordinary stir of sexual excitement consuming her. It was the deep and unsatisfied longing of love and desire which she knew even at this eleventh hour would have been the total commitment of her life, if she had ever been able to give herself to him.

Ending the kiss was the hardest thing

she had ever had to do, pulling away, her eyelids flicking slowly open as her lips missed his touch the moment they parted.

Her first thought was to escape, but he was too quick, pulling her back. 'Elissa, you're running away. What is it? Why not tell me the truth?'

She shook her head, her hair clinging in tendrils to her moist cheeks. 'It's nothing, Adam, please let me go.'

'If you want me to let you go, why allow me to kiss you like that?'

She shook her head, tensing as an aching pain grew inside her. 'I don't know. It was foolish of me.' She looked up at him reproachfully. 'And of you.'

His dark eyes flickered at the rebuke. 'One minute you want me gone from Larkhill, then the next you're in my arms and we're kissing and I can feel you responding to me . . . It's not my imagination.'

Her heart thudded, she knew that he was speaking the truth. But she could not admit her love for him, could not risk unbearable humiliation. 'You're making this almost impossible for me!' she cried bitterly, forcing her tears back behind her lids and blinking hard.

He looked down at her angrily. 'Why should I make it easy for you? You're the one who is dissatisfied, not me!'

She pushed away, angry herself now as she thought of Minty, and Adam's disregard for her trust as he tried now to prolong what must be for him a casual impulse. It was not much different from Philip's attitude when, imagining she was having an affair with Adam, he was still quite content to try his luck!

'I'm going back to Larkhill,' she croaked, wondering how a few moments in his arms could be so utterly annihilating to all her senses.

Her heart banged against her breast-bone as she began to turn, her eyes avoiding the frustrated gesture he made with his hands, thrusting them deeply into the well of his pockets.

'Are you coming?' she forced herself

to ask politely, a chill of foreboding going down her spine, knowing that now there was no turning back and she had closed the final chapters of their relationship as practice partners.

He gazed at her steadily with reproving eyes. 'What for?' she heard him mutter roughly. 'You can manage very well on your own. You don't need a partner. You only need Larkhill. I was a fool to think there was room for more in your life!'

She watched him walk in the opposite direction, her heart so heavy that she felt sick with grief. If only he knew. If only he understood what had happened to her since he had walked into her life. But even if he did, it wouldn't change his feeling for Minty. Long-time loves, like first loves, were almost impossible to compete with; she understood that much now.

11

Elissa bought a small posy of mixed flowers: freesias, chrysanthemums, tiny red roses and gypsophila, all her mother's favourites.

The cemetery was lively for a Tuesday morning. Four or five bicycles were harnessed with substantial locks to the iron railings, and children tiptoed in between the graves as their mothers placed tributes on the green hilly mounds or the polished concrete slabs.

Elissa had had butterflies last time she came. To her shame, she hadn't managed to stay more than a few minutes; the trauma had been too sharp, too vivid. Adam had just arrived at Larkhill then, she remembered. Her hopes had been high for the future.

She crouched down beside her parents' grave and arranged the flowers in a vase, filling it up with water from one of the cans. Then she brushed the headstone, her fingertips lingering over her parents' names.

'I'm sorry if I let you down, Dad,' she whispered huskily. 'I thought I was doing the right thing. I thought I'd made the right decision for Larkhill.'

Just the summer breeze blew around her, voices in her mind answering back, but it was only the breeze catching the heads of the flowers and lifting them.

She stayed a while, realising that her sense of grief was easing, just as it had done eventually after her mother's death, but then she'd had her father and they had comforted each other. With this thought, she realised that she had comfort this time too. Adam. He had made her drive the Land Rover and exorcise the ghost even her father could not deal with. He had cleared the surgery's debts and the practice was on its feet again. But falling in love with a man who was deeply in love with someone else . . . How could she have allowed that to happen?

Though Elissa had taken Tuesday morning off, she had determined to be back by two, in order to help Barbara with the weight-watching clinic. The first person Elissa bumped into was Mrs Preston, who, just after having Lavender weighed, was in raptures.

'She's lost three kilograms!' was the exultant cry and, as Elissa stood in the doorway, Mrs Preston hurried across Reception, her face beaming. 'Elissa, it's working! Lavender has actually lost weight, and me too!'

She saw that her client did indeed look slimmer. 'Well done!' she encouraged, bending to pat Lavender, who for once was not panting heavily. 'I was sure you'd both succeed.'

'Me too. Congratulations,' a deep voice said beside her, and Mrs Preston blushed under Adam's smile. Then, as the older woman turned to talk to the others, his dark eyes fell to Elissa. 'Yet another success. You must be very happy with what you've achieved.'

Elissa felt her throat tighten as she

met his deep gaze. 'Yes, I am,' she managed to answer with a weak smile. 'Are you joining us in the garden?'

He hesitated. 'No, I can't immediately. I've several clients due . . . But I did try looking for you earlier. I'd forgotten you'd booked the morning off.'

'I was long overdue to take flowers to the cemetery,' she explained briefly. 'Did you want to talk about something urgent?'

'Only as urgent as you want to make it. After what you told me last night . . . ' He shrugged, frowning. 'Listen — we can't talk here. It's my afternoon off tomorrow. Let's have lunch in the garden and try to get something resolved, shall we? After all, we can't go on for much longer now I know how you feel.'

Elissa nodded. 'All right. Tomorrow lunchtime.'

'Do you need any help this afternoon, by the way?' He glanced at his watch and she knew he would be awaiting the arrival of his own clients.

She shook her head. 'No. I'm giving Barbara a hand. But thanks all the same.'

As they parted, Elissa realised that she would have trouble in concentrating from now on, her anxiety growing as she wondered what kind of suggestions he was going to make. Would he be prepared to give up Larkhill or would he suggest that, as it was her wish to dissolve the partnership, she should leave? She could tell nothing from his expression and now, unfortunately, she would have to wait another day to find out.

The afternoon passed, though, surprisingly swiftly. Mrs Preston's achievement was not the only one. Wilbur the beagle, and Bonnie and Clyde, the golden retrievers, had also lost weight, while the rest of the class seemed to be unanimous in feeling that their pets' diet-sheets had arrested further weight gain.

'It just shows you what group therapy can do,' Barbara observed wryly at the end of the afternoon, as they brought in the chairs. 'There's a whisper among the women that they're going to set up their own slimming circle!'

Elissa laughed. 'With Mrs Preston as chairman, no doubt!'

Barbara giggled as she waved off the last client. 'Elissa, you look tired and a bit pale,' she commented as they finished the clearing. 'You're not overdoing things, I hope?'

Elissa hesitated, tempted briefly to share her problems with someone who might understand, but the moment passed, and with a big effort she smiled cheerfully. 'Oh, no! Quite the opposite, Barbara, you're making my life a lot easier now.'

The nurse looked appeased. 'I hope so! Things really do seem to be taking off for Larkhill, don't they?'

Elissa nodded, knowing that with Adam's energies and skill Larkhill would always be assured of success, and for one moment she tried to picture herself gone from the scene. Would anyone miss her? Would the clients even notice? Would this place — the sum total of her life and work — be any the worse off for her absence?

Preferring not to answer her own question, Elissa put the whole business from her mind for the rest of the evening and, after a busy surgery the following morning, discovered that she had managed not to think about either Adam or her future until just before lunch, when her nerves seemed to catch up with her. She found herself tensing as she walked into the sunny garden, carrying a tray of iced lemonade and chicken salad sandwiches by courtesy of Grace.

Her heart leapt at the sight of Adam, already seated at the patio table. He stood up to help her with the tray and, as he took it from her, she noticed how lean and fit he looked in a white T-shirt and dark green Bermuda shorts, with flip-flops on his large brown feet.

'Please help yourself,' she said coolly as she poured drinks. Dressed in her working clothes — a shirtwaister blouse and navy skirt — she felt rather formal, but there was no time to change as she had only three quarters of an hour left for lunch.

Adam munched on a sandwich, though she could see he really wasn't hungry. Finally he gave up the attempt and turned his dark eyes on her. 'Elissa, are you still of the same opinion as you were on Monday?' he asked tightly.

She nodded, her heart hammering.

'You want me to leave Larkhill — '

'Or,' Elissa interrupted huskily, 'the alternative is that I leave.'

He shook his head, frowning deeply. 'I can't believe you'd do that just to escape our partnership.'

She sighed, chewing on her bottom lip. Was this going to be another dreadful emotional wrangle? She didn't think she could bear another scene, and she was just about to say so when he shrugged, his lips compressing tightly together. 'I've a proposition to put to you. No . . . don't worry, I'm not going to try to change your mind.' He hesitated, drawing a circle idly with his finger on the table. 'I simply want you to think about it, very seriously, for a few more days. If, by the end of the weekend, you still feel the same, I'll agree to leave.'

She felt her jaw drop as she stared at him in astonishment. 'You mean — '

'I mean if you can look me in the eye and tell me truthfully you want me out of your life, I'll go.'

Elissa sat wordless. This was the last thing she had imagined he would say!

'The deal includes you coming with me to Peter and Helen's on Saturday, by the way,' he remarked, almost as an afterthought.

Elissa frowned. 'But surely not now! Adam, it would be a terribly uncomfortable evening . . . '

He nodded, his facial expression unchanging. 'Maybe it will. However, those are my terms. Do you accept them?'

How could she not? It was all she had

wanted. She looked into his dark eyes. 'Yes, I accept.'

He sat in silence, his finger still trailing aimlessly over the table-top. Then he arose, gave her a stiff nod and said, 'Well, you must finish your lunch. I think we've said all there is to say.'

Elissa watched him leave, tall and broad-shouldered, walking with long strides, his athletically built body moving gracefully under the casual summer clothes. Her heart was aching, aching so deeply that she wanted to cry. And yet, she reflected with dismay, she had her wish, didn't she?

★ ★ ★

The next two days passed in an uneasy but amicable truce. Elissa made no mention of the conversation to Adam when she saw him; in fact their communication was limited to medical issues apart from their brief meetings in the morning at Grace's breakfast-table.

She was less comfortable, though,

when she found herself gritting her teeth on Friday evening as the white Porsche drew alongside Adam's Mercedes outside Larkhill. Elissa made sure that she was last to leave the surgery, eliminating the chance of bumping into anyone as she went into the house.

She did hear voices from above later that evening, and perhaps the sound of music coming from one of the open windows. And on Adam's late walk around the garden with Arnie, there were two figures . . .

Elissa closed her bedroom curtains swiftly before the strollers thought they were being overlooked. Was it Minty walking with him? Were they embracing in the quiet night? Was Adam kissing Minty as he had kissed her?

Tormented by her imagination, she finally went to bed, wishing above all that she could avoid the ridiculous event of tomorrow night. Why Adam should want to insist on what would be, certainly for her, an awkward and embarrassing evening, she had no idea, except maybe the obscure recovery of male pride he felt he had lost in the collapse of their partnership. Or perhaps something even more personal? What if Adam and Minty were going to take the opportunity to announce their re-engagement . . . ?

* * *

Elissa spent Saturday in Farwell. She had no idea why she was being so extravagant and why she had bought such a beautiful dress, but when she slipped it on that evening, and slid her hands over the figure-hugging jade-coloured crêpe, she knew she hadn't wasted her time in searching for just the right dress.

Her tawny skin against the colour was perfect. The jade matched her eyes, and the small jade pendants she wore in her ears sparkled when they caught the light. Her fashionable shoes, with delicate heels, set off her slender curves as she turned around before the mirror, wondering what to do with her thick, glinting hair, extra-wavy after being washed, and streaked with natural golden highlights.

When the knock came on her door, she realised that there was no time to do anything! She hurried to open it, expecting to see Adam. She had a shock when Philip stood there, grinning.

'You look fantastic!' he said, whistling through his teeth.

'Thank you.' She looked into the hall, avoiding his intimate gaze. 'Where are the others?'

He shrugged, looking very trendy in a light grey suit, waves of expensive aftershave wafting through her door. 'I've been told to wait down here. Minty can't stand me pacing around the flat.'

Elissa suspected that Philip had been conveniently got rid of again. She could hardly send him away. 'You'd better come in then,' she offered politely, making sure that she left the door open as he walked through and down the hall into her drawing-room.

'Would you like a drink?' she asked, hoping Minty and Adam wouldn't take all night.

'Love one. Scotch on the rocks, please.'

Elissa gave him a rueful smile. 'You're not driving, obviously!'

He laughed, his blue eyes twinkling. 'No. I'm going to enjoy myself instead.'

Elissa poured a small version of what he had asked for. She was beginning to feel nervous as he watched her trying to clip a pendant around her neck.

'Here, let me,' he said, downing his drink in one gulp. Elissa let him take the chain, and held up her hair for him to complete the delicate operation.

As he moved clumsily over her, she felt rather than saw the movement across the room.

'Adam . . . I didn't see you there,' she gasped, wondering how long he had been watching.

'The door was open,' he muttered, clearly unamused.

'Philip was just . . . ' She gave up her explanation as she could see he had already chosen to think the worst. She dragged the chain from Philip's hand and decided she would dispense with it altogether, slipping the pendant into a drawer. 'Are you ready to go?' she asked, collecting her purse.

'If you two are.' He frowned at the glass in the other man's hand.

'Why don't you let me drive?' Philip suggested sarcastically. 'My car's faster.'

Elissa realised that he was already a little drunk. Not obviously, but his voice held a note of carelessness in it, even challenge, which seemed directed towards Adam.

Adam ignored the offer, stonily frowning at Elissa. She grabbed her key from the table, thinking the night already had all the hallmarks of a disaster! She was almost relieved when Minty appeared, though after her initial relief her heart sank, for Minty looked stunning. Wearing her hair up in a chignon, she had tied a black velvet choker around her

318

slender neck, and her red dress left nothing to the imagination as it clung to her curvaceous body.

'You look enchanting,' Philip said flatly, as she stood there.

'What a cosy scene!' Minty observed, gazing at the three of them.

Elissa tried to smile brightly as she led the way out, but as she took one last look at Arnie as he nosed his way to Adam's side for a last stroke, she wished with all her heart that she was staying here at Larkhill with him.

★ ★ ★

Peter Sharp had trained with Adam and, together with his wife Helen, welcomed Adam and his guests. Their country house lay north of Larkhill, a beautiful Georgian building with huge rooms and a swirling staircase.

'I stayed with Peter and Helen for a week or two when I came back from the States,' Adam explained after the introductions were over. 'I think it was then I decided I would like to settle in this part of the world.'

Elissa caught Minty's expression of boredom. Obviously she did not feel the same empathy with Shropshire, and there was a tense silence as Helen spoke quickly to lighten the atmosphere.

'Adam was so fortunate to come across Larkhill,' Peter's wife remarked. 'Lucky man!'

Helen had a sweet, cherubic face with clear grey eyes, and Elissa smiled warmly back. She liked Adam's friends, and she talked for a while with Helen about Larkhill as Philip and Minty and Adam were introduced to other guests by Peter. Minty slid a possessive hand under Adam's arm, and suddenly Elissa felt very glad of Helen's company.

An hour or so later, despite having shaken a dozen hands and talked with other vets until she felt that every conceivable technique had been thrashed black and blue, Elissa found her eyes wandering to Adam across the crowded room. Minty stood at his side in the red dress, tossing back her lovely black hair and laughing.

Loving him from afar was even more difficult than she had imagined it would be, she thought miserably, as she tried to discuss a new drug being tested for tumour treatment. How would she feel when he was no longer part of her life at all?

But at last, diverting her thoughts, Helen came to her rescue, dragging her to the buffet-table. 'Come and have some food, Elissa, and tell me more about Larkhill.'

Elissa obligingly sampled the delicious food, trying to work up an appetite. Managing to talk about Adam's referral unit, she felt she wasn't doing so badly — that was, until Philip appeared beside her. Unfortunately, at the very same moment, the lights dimmed and soft music began to play in another room. Helen was whisked away, and Elissa realised that she was marooned with Philip.

'Come and dance,' he coaxed and,

taking her hand, he pulled her towards the music. As she could do nothing without drawing attention, she prayed he would behave himself. But as soon as they began to dance it became clear that she had cause for concern.

His arms closed around her like manacles.

'You've had too much to drink,' she reproved in a firm whisper, trying to loosen his grip.

'At the moment I don't much care,' he muttered, hanging on to her. 'Tell me, did you know it was Adam who broke off the engagement with Minty?'

Hit with this thunderbolt, Elissa looked up at him incredulously. 'You must be mistaken, Philip,' she mumbled, flustered. 'Minty told me — '

'Minty wanted you to think he still held a torch for her, which he doesn't,' her companion sneered spitefully. 'You see, you thought exactly what Minty wanted you to think — you fell into her little trap.' He swayed as he tried to pull her closer. 'After the trouble I made, I thought I had better do my good deed for the day and warn you.' But quickly bored with his good deed, he shrugged and gave a laugh. 'Oh, come on, who gives a damn? Let's finish our dance.' He jerked her towards him and she almost lost her footing.

She was saved by a pair of strong hands around her waist, and a decisive arm snapped discreetly in between her and Philip.

'You're going home, old man,' Adam said, taking Philip's shoulder firmly and easing him away from Elissa. 'I've ordered a taxi.'

'I don't want a taxi,' Philip protested, looking indignant. 'I want to dance.'

'I wouldn't argue until you've sobered up,' Adam warned him grimly. 'Then, if you want to pick any bones, I'll be quite happy to help you do just that.'

With a warning glance at Elissa, Adam slipped the palm of his hand under Philip's elbow and firmly steered him off the floor. Trying to piece together what Philip had said, Elissa threaded her way through the dancers until she reached a quiet corner.

'Is your friend under the weather?' Helen asked, coming up with a tray of sherry.

Elissa hesitated. 'I'm sorry, did anyone notice?'

Helen laughed. 'Not a soul. I'm glad to say everyone's enjoying themselves too much. Do you think he'll be all right?'

'Oh, yes, Adam's helping him.'

Helen grinned. 'I'd better circulate. See you later.'

Was what Philip said true? Elissa wondered as she stood watching the dancers, and then, making her jump, a hand slid around her waist.

'Come along with me,' Adam commanded in a low whisper, almost lifting her off her feet, and, whirling her past the dancers, he propelled her through the long windows which led out to the terrace.

'Where are we going?' Elissa found herself being thrust between the empty chairs and tables, until finally they could go no further without being lost in the garden.

'You're the most annoying, stubborn, single-minded woman I've ever come across in my life!' he growled as he twisted her to face him. 'Now, I want to hear,' he added more slowly, 'your true reasons for breaking up our partnership!'

Elissa began to stammer. 'I . . . I . . . thought . . . '

'You thought what?' he prodded, with an angry frown. 'Remember, this time, the truth!'

'I thought you were still in love with Minty,' she admitted, as her face turned scarlet. 'Then Philip told me this evening that it wasn't Minty who broke off your engagement, but you . . . and I began to think — '

'Which is more than half your trouble,' he cut in as he gazed down at her with a frustrated sigh. 'Thinking all the wrong things and imagining far worse.' He pulled her to him, his mouth forming into a gentle smile. 'Elissa Hart, I'm not letting you go until I've kissed all those ridiculous ideas out of your head and put some new ones in there!'

Then suddenly she was in his arms, her breasts crushed against him, his mouth covering hers again and again with deep, passionate kisses, strong hands curving round her shoulders, the warmth of her skin burning against his fingers as he touched her soft cheeks.

'You little fool! You stubborn, independent, silly little fool,' he whispered huskily. 'You've fought me all along. Don't you know I love you? That I'm hopelessly, madly, desperately in love with you?'

She stared at him in disbelief, hearing the words as though she were in a dream. A wonderful, incredible, unbelievable dream.

'Of course I love you and not Minty!' His hands moved down her back, possessing her slender body as they met at her waist, holding her tenderly. 'I wanted so many times to tell you!' He grinned as he kissed her nose. 'When I first met you, my instinct told me you were suspicious of my motives. What chance had I of trying to make you believe in me? I was long over Minty, probably because I had never been in love with her in the first place and, thank God, I had the sense to call the engagement off before she came to the States.'

'But . . . but she loves you!' Elissa blurted out. 'She told me she intended to have you and I . . . I believed every word.'

He frowned at her askance. 'Minty loves Minty, surely you know that by now? She likes the sound of being a consultant's wife but, as you saw, she'd run a mile if a limping dog came within twenty yards of her!' He laughed as his eyes twinkled. 'I must admit, convincing her of the fact is rather more difficult. And you didn't help very much, always disappearing when your company would have been the ideal solution to my problem.'

Elissa gasped. 'You mean you wanted me to be around?'

'Of course I did!' He looked at her in surprise. 'My plan began to backfire when you made it plain you hated the sight of me! And to make matters worse, I really thought you'd taken a liking to Philip.'

Elissa shook her head numbly. 'But I overheard the call you took on the night you came to dinner! You tried to persuade Minty not to bring Philip to Larkhill. You wanted to see her alone!'

He threw back his head with a bitter groan. 'So that's what was wrong with you that night? Oh, you silly little witch! Why didn't you say?' He stroked the hair from her face, cupping her head in his hands. 'I didn't want Philip to come to Larkhill simply because I've never trusted the man. I preferred him not to be involved in what I had to say. I liked him even less when he started showing an interest in you!'

'But I saw her in your arms, I saw you — '

Adam tipped up her chin to gaze into her doubtful green eyes. 'Oh, you of little faith!' he whispered, shaking his dark head. 'Minty used every opportunity to create the wrong impression and you obviously fell for it. I just couldn't win. Finally, I was so fed up with the situation I decided to take her out to dinner, in full view of the public — where I was safe — and politely but firmly tell her our relationship had ended the day I broke off our engagement and there was no point in her thinking otherwise.'

Elissa suddenly had a mental picture of that night. 'And then you came home to find — '

'To find Philip kissing you in the car, which gave Minty the opportunity to play the scene for all it was worth.'

'Oh, Adam, it looked awful, I know, but it wasn't what it seemed . . . I promise you . . . '

He nodded, a wry smile on his face. 'I was jealous as hell.'

'Were you? Oh, I'm so pleased,' she

sighed, wanting to laugh and cry at the same time.

'You little idiot.' His deep voice caught in his throat. Bringing down his dark head to her lips, kissing him with the pent-up passion she had saved for so long, she let the wanton ache of repressed longing flow freely inside her.

When at last they surfaced, Elissa was breathless. He held her tightly, staring at the tender moonlit beauty of her face. 'Let's go home,' he whispered. 'I want you all to myself.'

'But where is Minty?' Elissa murmured uneasily, suddenly conscious of her absence, wondering if she might spring from the shadows.

Adam smiled ruefully. 'I sent her off with Philip. After all, the man needed a helping hand.'

Elissa kissed Helen's cheek as they made their discreet farewells. Their hosts, if they had noted the intrigue, gave no sign as they said goodbye.

The Mercedes stood in the moonlight and Elissa smiled, reflecting that the drive home through the night would be very different from the one coming, when there had been four of them in the car and she had been dreading the evening ahead.

The journey was slow, rhythmic, almost as though Adam was gently giving them both time for what was to come.

Then Larkhill appeared in the darkness.

'Alone at last,' he sighed as the engine faded to silence.

Elissa heard an owl hoot as she climbed out of the car, hardly on her feet before Adam was beside her. 'No Porsche,' he said quietly, 'which means they've left. I imagine Minty would prefer the drive back to London tonight rather than face us in the morning.'

'Us?' Elissa frowned.

'I told her I was in love with you, that I'd been in love with you since the very first day I'd come to Larkhill.'

Elissa felt the tears spring to her eyes. 'Oh, Adam!'

'Let's stop talking about other people,' he whispered throatily as he took her in his arms, 'and talk about us.'

'Adam!' she gasped, as the mention of other people made her think of her godfather. 'I've asked Harry for a loan! He thinks — '

His deep chuckle prevented her from completing her sentence. 'Do you honestly think Harry was taken in by the story of the avenging fiancée? No, he had more sense than to believe you, I'm happy to say, and he called me up. We had quite a long chat about a certain young lady who had got herself into a pickle and needed sorting out.'

'You knew!' she croaked in surprise. 'You knew all the time! You've put me through agony this week, even letting me think you would leave Larkhill!'

'A man has to have a little revenge,' he grinned. 'If you had told me the real reason for wanting to buy me out, then of course, I could have swept you into my arms and carried you indoors . . . as I'm going to now . . . '

No sooner had he said this than he slipped his hands under her, drawing her up to the safety of his hard chest. Under Larkhill's eaves he kissed her in the moonlight as she whispered breathlessly, 'I love you so, Adam.'

'And I didn't believe I'd ever hear you say it,' he murmured, as Arnie began to bark. 'Say it again for me.'

A warm flush of anticipation crept into her cheeks. 'I love you . . . I love you!'

'Can we arrange for this conversation to be held on a more permanent basis?' he asked, smiling wickedly in the darkness.

'How permanent?' she asked, as her heart stood still.

'Not a day less,' he said softly, kissing her again, 'than every day for the rest of our lives.'

THE END

Other titles in the
Linford Romance Library:

SURGEON IN PORTUGAL

Anna Ramsay

'A strong dose of sunshine' is the prescription for Nurse Liz Larking, recovering from glandular fever. And a villa in the Algarve seems the ideal place to recuperate, even if it means cooking for the villa's owner, eminent cardiac surgeon Hugh Forsythe: brilliant, caring, awe-inspiring — and dangerously easy to fall in love with. Liz soon realises that this doctor is more potent than any virus — and ironically, it seems he could just as easily break a heart as cure one . . .

CINDERELLA SRN

Anna Ramsay

Despite her tender years, Student Nurse Kate Cameron is like a mother hen, forever worrying about her patients and her family. So it's a huge joke when her friends transform her into a *femme fatale* for the hospital's Christmas Ball. The joke backfires though, when Kate finds herself falling in love . . . But what chance is there of a fairy-tale ending when this Cinderella has chapped hands and an unflattering uniform, and Prince Charming turns out to be Luke Harvey, the new senior registrar?

A VERY SPECIAL GIRL

Renee Shann

Though warned by her parents, Emma marries Nicholas Stagger, a Krasnovian from Traj. Too late she has found that her parents were right, for Nicky's infidelities are more than she can stand. Furthermore, Nicky's involvement in the politics of his own country brings Emma herself into danger; but it is through this involvement that she meets Paul, President of Krasnovia. At last Emma can see her future clearly, but danger still awaits . . .

NORTH BY NORTHEAST

Phyllis Humphrey

Haley Parsons, a school teacher on her first real vacation in years, boards the beautiful and luxurious American Orient Express for a week-long train excursion from New Orleans to Washington, D.C. But then her jewelry begins to disappear and she finds herself an unwitting player in a kidnapping and robbery attempt. The culprit is evidently aboard the train; and Jonathan Shafer, Haley's handsome, newfound love interest, is somehow involved. Who is he, really? And what part will he play in all this?